SIEGE
AT THE
GATES

Other books by Thurman C. Petty, Jr.:

The Temple Gates:
Josiah Purges Judah's Idolatry

Fire in the Gates:
The Drama of Jeremiah and the Fall of Judah

Gate of the Gods:
God's Quest for Nebuchadnezzar

The Open Gates:
From Babylon's Ashes, Freedom for the Jews

The Flood

To order,
call
1-800-765-6955.

Visit us at
www.reviewandherald.com
for information on other Review and Herald® products.

SIEGE
AT THE
GATES

The Story of Hezekiah and Sennacherib

THURMAN C. PETTY, JR.

Autumn
House® Publishing
www.autumnhousepublishing.com
A Division of **REVIEW AND HERALD® PUBLISHING**
Since 1861

Published by Autumn House® Publishing, a division of Review and Herald® Publishing, Hagerstown, MD 21741-1119

Autumn House® titles may be purchased in bulk for educational, business, fund-raising, or sales promotional use. For information, please e-mail SpecialMarkets@ reviewandherald.com.

Autumn House® Publishing publishes biblically based materials for spiritual, physical, and mental growth and Christian discipleship.

The author assumes full responsibility for the accuracy of all facts and quotations as cited in this book.

Bible texts credited to Jerusalem are from *The Jerusalem Bible,* copyright © 1966 by Darton, Longman & Todd, Ltd., and Doubleday & Company, Inc. Used by permission of the publisher.

This book was
Edited by Gerald Wheeler
Cover design by Trent Truman
Cover art by Thiago Lobo
Electronic makeup by Shirley M. Bolivar
Typeset: 11.5/13.5 Bembo

PRINTED IN U.S.A.

11 10 09 08 07   5 4 3 2 1

Library of Congress Cataloging-in-Publication Data
Petty, Thurman C., 1940-   .
   Siege at the gates : the story of Hezekiah and Sennacherib / Thurman C. Petty, Jr.
         p. cm.
   ISBN 978-0-8127-0441-9
   1. Hezekiah, King of Judah—Fiction.   2. Sennacherib, King of Assyria, d. 681 B.C.—Fiction.   3. Bible. O.T.—History of Biblical events—Fiction.   4. Israel—Kings and rulers—Fiction.   5. Assyria—Kings and rulers—Fiction. I. Title
   PS3566.E894S54 2007
   813'.54—dc22

                                                    2006102906

Dedication

To my wife, Martha,
and to my daughter, Lydia,
who enthusiastically helped me
in the writing of this book.

Contents

A Chronology of Hezekiah's Time

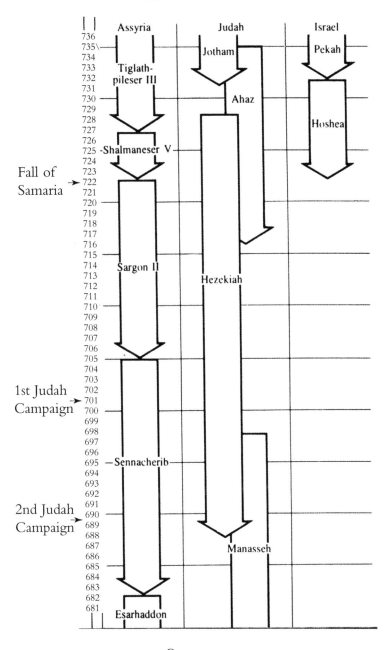

Chapter 1

A Stranger in Sackcloth

The blare of ram's-horn trumpets filled the air as Judah's victorious troops approached Jerusalem, returning from a foray into Philistia, Israel's ancient enemy. Thousands of cheering people lined the city walls, waving palm branches and praising God for the soldiers' safe return. As they marched along, King Hezekiah surveyed them. The four black mares that drew his royal chariot, sensing the spirit of the occasion, pranced in unison. The swords, shields, and helmets of the infantry gleamed in the sun.

Behind Hezekiah galloped the cavalry. Their shields were smaller than those of the infantry, and each man rode a choice, battle-hardened Egyptian horse. Next came the battle chariots, each pulled by two swift steeds and carrying a driver and an archer. The wheels had long-bladed knives, sharpened to a razor-edge, fastened to the spokes. The chariots would rush through the enemy's ranks, cutting them to shreds. Hezekiah remembered how effective they had been against the city of Ekron.

"I've wanted independence from Assyria all my life," the king smiled to his charioteer. "So I've declared Judah's freedom from Assyria by conquering Ekron. Now all of Palestine will follow me. We'll see if Assyria dares face my veteran armies."

Hezekiah glanced at the prisoners chained to his chariot. For a moment he pitied the men and women who would become slaves in Jerusalem, but then he shrugged. All conquering generals returned with a train of captives to prove their prowess. King Padi led the motley group.

The royal chariot entered the city gate and rumbled down the street. Hezekiah smiled at the throngs of well-wishers lining the street, but his mind wandered to other times. Seeing the familiar street, the people, the houses, the Temple gate, suddenly he found himself transported back through the years. Yes, he had walked down this very street . . . with his mother . . . going to the Temple . . . to a coronation for his father.

Old King Jotham planned to crown his son Ahaz as king to rule beside himself. The royal party marched through the palace gates to the thunder of 10,000 voices chanting, "Long live the king! Long live the king!"

The king and his son led the royal family—wives, concubines, children in great number, and countless servants. Abijah, Ahaz's vibrant young wife, followed near the rear of the parade, keeping an eye on her 6-year-old son, Hezekiah. The daughter of high priest Zechariah, she had often dreamed of the day when she would become queen of Yahweh's people. Only her love for her Creator exceeded her fondness for her husband and son.

She remembered her father joyfully enacting the tales of Yahweh's triumphs on behalf of Judah and Israel before the great schism. But she returned to the present when she saw the Temple gates. The procession entered and the official Levite heralds sounded the rams' horns. The shrill blast of a dozen horns rose above the shouting chants of the multitude, and the crowd elbowed into the outer court.

The coronation would occur on the Temple porch, for the new king needed Yahweh's blessing. For generations the people had followed the ways of their neighbors, worshipping pagan deities at the many high places throughout the country. Yet tradition still bound them by slender cords to the one true God—Yahweh, Creator of all.

A hush fell over the throng as King Jotham climbed the Temple steps. Standing beside one of the giant bronze pillars, he extended his scepter to the people in a gesture of royal goodwill.

Hezekiah peered at his grandfather. He liked the old man. The royal robes that hung to his feet, the crown that sparkled with gold, silver, and multicolored jewels, and the signet ring on his finger—all showed his authority as ruler of Judah.

The boy's father waited at the foot of the stairs. Except for the absence of the crown and signet ring—which rested on an ornate pillow held by one of the priests—Ahaz was dressed like the king.

"I can hardly wait to see the crown upon Father's head," he whispered to his mother.

"Me too," she smiled, squeezing his hand.

His gaze moving beyond his father, the boy's eyes explored the crowds. Everyone had dressed in his or her finest clothing. The women wore one-piece, close-fitting dresses, gathered at the waist with tie cords. Their skirts hung straight to the ankles, hemmed just above their sandaled feet. Some of the dresses displayed embroidered multicolored designs. Over their shoulders many wore a veil-like shawl that dropped to their knees. Most of the women seemed heavy with jewelry: earrings, necklaces, bands of gold around the ankles, gold rings in their noses, dozens of bracelets on their arms, and gold threads running through their hair. Absently the boy wondered how they could possibly be comfortable like that.

Suddenly Hezekiah spotted a man who stood out among the rest of the crowd. Instead of fine linen, jewels, and glowing royal robes, he wore a rough garment of sackcloth with a wide leather belt. His crude sandals revealed his bony feet, and his face seemed more peaceful and kinder than the others.

Siege at the Gates

Young Hezekiah stared at the stranger on the far side of the court. *He hasn't dressed up like the others,* the prince thought to himself. And yet no one asked him to leave. Apparently he belonged here in the Temple. The boy became so enthralled by the strange man that he almost missed the coronation service. But Abijah brought her child back to attention by a quick squeeze of the hand. Glancing toward the porch, he spotted his father kneeling on the top step. The high priest read Yahweh's law to the king. Handing the scroll to another priest, he slowly poured fragrant anointing oil onto the head of the crown prince. The king then set the diadem upon the head of his son.

Rising, Ahaz stood with his father beside the bronze pillar. The old monarch's voice rang clear and strong, proclaiming his son as king of Judah. And the people thundered their echo: "Long live the king!"

The crowd then followed the royal pair back to the palace, where Ahaz occupied the throne of David. But Hezekiah remembered little else of that day. His child's mind couldn't follow the different ceremonies. Throughout the day his thoughts kept returning to the stranger in sackcloth. He determined to discover the man's identity as soon as possible.

The day's activities ended, and evening shrouded the city. The crowds dispersed, and the two kings retired to their council chambers. A servant girl dressed Hezekiah in his nightshirt, then Abijah told him his bedtime story. But the child was restless.

His mother at first assumed that his behavior was a reaction to the coronation. But she soon discovered that another matter plagued his active mind.

"Mother," the boy said when the story was over, "I saw a strange man in the Temple today."

"You did?" Abijah smiled. "What did he look like?"

"Well, he didn't dress like everybody else. He wore sack-cloth with a leather belt. Did you see him?"

"Yes, Hezekiah. I saw him. And I know him well."

"You do?" The young prince's excitement grew. "Mother, who is he?"

"Isaiah the prophet. He teaches our people to know and love Yahweh."

"A prophet! Oh, Mother. May I meet him someday? Maybe Isaiah will tell me how Yahweh speaks to him."

Abijah stroked the curly, jet-black hair of her son. She remembered her own first meeting with Isaiah. "He is a close relative," she explained. "I've known him since I was a little girl. Isaiah always seemed sensitive to spiritual things, but after his vision in the Temple some years ago, he has been a powerful preacher. And you want to meet him?"

"Yes, Mother. May I?"

"Of course you may! Now listen," she said, "tomorrow we will have more ceremonies as part of the coronation. But on the day after tomorrow, I will take you to meet the prophet." Abijah smoothed her son's pillow and sleeping mat and prodded him toward it. "But tonight, you must go to sleep." Pulling his blanket up under his chin, she kissed him goodnight.

Mother and son, accompanied by a royal guard, went out through the palace grounds and into Jerusalem itself. Houses lined both sides of the narrow streets. Every available space had been used for building sites. Some people had constructed their homes on top of others, sometimes even over-hanging the street to join others extending from the opposite side to form a bridge.

The street they followed climbed a hill, turned a corner, and then descended down a steep flight of steps into the potter's quarter. Hezekiah had never imagined that the vases and pitchers of the palace had once been soft clay in a potter's hands. He stared in fascination as the men shaped new vessels. But his mother's gentle tug reminded him that their destination lay elsewhere.

They passed into the market. People crowded through the streets, stopping at stalls to make purchases. A child could easily get lost in the press, so Abijah tightly grasped his hand. The throng and Hezekiah's frequent stops to gaze at the merchants chanting their wares greatly slowed their pace. Here an Arab haggled over the price of a saddle; there a grain merchant weighed an ephah of wheat for a stooped old woman; up ahead a wealthy woman studied the jewels offered by a Phoenician merchant from Sidon; and to one side a man tried on a new tunic from Babylon. There were so many things to see and to do at the bazaar. But they must hurry on.

Rounding another corner, they descended more steps and slipped into a passageway beside the city wall. Finally they paused before a rough-hewn wooden door.

Abijah knocked, and a woman in her mid twenties opened the door. "Oh!" gasped the woman. "Queen Abijah! I never expected you. Do come in!" She bowed and stepped aside as she swung her hand toward the interior of her home.

Leaving the guard in the street, Abijah nudged Hezekiah to enter ahead of her. The boy's eyes took a minute or two to get used to the darkness. He could see several olive oil lamps casting soft shadows around the room. The main room served as living room, dining room, bedroom, and guest room. The prince mentally contrasted Isaiah's dwelling with the light, spacious, multicolored rooms of the palace.

"I wish I had known you were coming," the woman exclaimed.

"Hezekiah wants to meet your husband," Abijah explained. "He saw Isaiah at the coronation and has talked of nothing else since."

"I expect my husband back any time now. Won't you sit

16

down?" She motioned toward the only two stools in the room.

The boy could now see many details that he had missed when he first came in from the sunlit street. The dark, gray stucco walls bore no designs of any kind. One high small square window opened onto a tiny courtyard behind the house. A lamp and a partially opened scroll rested on a table at one end of the main room. *The priests read from scrolls like that,* Hezekiah thought. *It must be a part of the Torah—the books of Moses.*

Just as he was about to ask about the scroll Isaiah stepped into the room. Daylight streamed over the man's shoulder, casting harsh shadows across his bearded face. The prophet appeared much younger than he had at the Temple—not more than about 25.

"Well, what have we here?" The man's deep, mellow voice revealed surprise and delight. The boy couldn't remember ever hearing a happier voice. He liked the man of God.

"Hezekiah, would you like to meet my two sons?"

"Sure." The thought of new playmates delighted the prince.

"They're younger than you are," the prophet said as he led the boy into the courtyard. Two small boys played in one corner. Hezekiah guessed that they must be about 2 and 4 years of age.

Patting one of the boys on the head, Isaiah introduced him. "My son, I'd like you to meet Hezekiah, the crown prince. And, Hezekiah, this is Shear-jashub." He set the older boy on his lap while explaining the name. "Yahweh has revealed that Judah will pass through hard times. Enemies may even take the people away. But God will bring back a remnant to their own land."

"I hope I'm one of those in the remnant," Hezekiah said.

"So do I." Then retrieving his second son, he stated, "This is Maher-shalal-hash-baz. And his name means, 'If

17

Judah continues to forget Yahweh, He will hasten their doom.' "

Hezekiah's voice choked. "But what can happen to Judah when Yahweh has promised to protect it?"

Isaiah's eyes moistened. "Judah has strayed far from Yahweh. But God has called you, Hezekiah, to become king one day. You must lead our nation back to its Creator."

The prince's lips started to form words, but they stopped in his throat. *The prophet wants me to lead Judah back to God?* he wondered.

At last his voice returned. "I didn't know our people had left Yahweh. But if they have," he determined, "then I will lead them back. May Yahweh help me."

"Yes," agreed Isaiah, patting the prince on the head, "Yahweh will help you."

Chapter 2

A Baby in Flames

Hezekiah couldn't believe his ears. "It doesn't seem possible that Grandpa Jotham is dead!" he cried.

But alas, the king had indeed died, and sorrow draped the palace. Every servant and palace official prepared for the funeral, for Jewish law required that a person be buried before sunset. Messengers carried the news throughout the kingdom, and crowds gathered at the palace gate, clothed in sackcloth.

Late in the afternoon the procession filed through the palace gates toward the royal burial grounds on the Mount of Olives. Jotham's monumental sepulcher dwarfed most of the other tombs on the hillside.

Young Hezekiah marveled as he saw old and young, rich and poor, pass by the bier to salute their fallen monarch. He glanced up at his mother and hugged her with all the strength of his nine years. "I guess, now that Grandfather Jotham is dead, Isaiah will be my closest friend."

The ceremonies finally ended, and for several minutes the mother and son walked quietly side by side down the steep road into the Kidron Valley. As they approached the little bridge over the tiny stream, Hezekiah tugged on his mother's skirt, and the two stopped. Tears streaked both their faces.

"Mother," the boy sobbed, "I wish Father were as kind as Grandfather." The moment the words escaped his lips, he put his hand to his mouth, knowing he should have never expressed such thoughts. But the pained look in his mother's eyes told him that she agreed.

Darkness fell over the city, matching the gloom each citizen felt. The wailing ceased as the people turned to their sleeping mats. But sleep at first eluded Hezekiah.

"Mother," he inquired as she tucked him again into bed, "why do people die?"

"Do you remember the story of Adam, and how death entered the world because of sin?"

"Yes."

"Well, death comes to everyone some time." She dabbed a handkerchief at the tearstains on the child's face. "But death will not always reign."

"It won't?"

"No. Yahweh promises that all who serve Him faithfully and believe in the coming of His Messiah will join His kingdom that will never end . . . in which no one will ever die."

"Are you sure, Mother?" The boy raised himself on one elbow.

"Yes, dear, I'm sure. Isaiah has told me about it many times. But you must sleep now, my child. God's kingdom will come in His own good time."

Hezekiah's eyes closed, and now he fell asleep so quickly that Abijah marveled at it.

Almost immediately trouble struck the kingdom of Ahaz. A runner from the north gasped out his message. Crowds flocked around him at the palace gate, but they couldn't understand him.

"Stop!" A palace guard held up his hand. "I think you should tell the king first." He led the trembling man toward the palace.

King Ahaz received the messenger at once. The man threw himself on his face before the king, but the Judahite ruler commanded him to rise.

"My lord"—he had caught his breath now—"the kings of Israel and Syria have joined together to fight against Judah.

They plan to raid our country . . . to carry away our people . . . to plunder our cities." Shaking violently from fear and exhaustion, he broke into sobs.

Ahaz paled, his mind racing to understand his predicament. Obviously his neighbors wanted to attack before he could fully organize. After a moment of silence, he regained his composure. "Reward the runner for his faithful service," he ordered to an official standing beside him. "Send for my counselors. We have not a minute to spare."

The palace sprang to life as servants rushed to fulfill their master's bidding. Soon men gathered in the royal chambers, each asking the other what the emergency could mean.

Within minutes the room vibrated with tense emotion as everyone gathered around the throne. Something must be done, and fast. But what? The armies could not be more than a day from Jerusalem.

The sun was not yet visible over the Mount of Olives, but already King Ahaz had led his army out through the city gates. He wanted to meet the enemy away from Jerusalem, for the city was not ready for a siege. But it was already too late. The invaders' advance patrols had reached the summit of the Mount of Olives. Within minutes the armies hurled themselves at one another, and cries of pain shattered the air as soldiers on both sides fell wounded and dying.

The battle seesawed for hours until the dead and injured littered the slopes of the Kidron Valley. The king's brother, chamberlain, and leading general all perished. The invaders outnumbered Judah's troops on every side. The king himself barely escaped death several times.

Realizing that the battle was lost, Ahaz signaled retreat. His troops fought a courageous rearguard action as the king led the small remnant of his battered army into the city. Only a hail of arrows from the top of the wall prevented the enemy from following them into Jerusalem.

Bruised and exhausted, Ahaz summoned his surviving counselors to decide their next step. The loss of several able officers had decreased their numbers. They sat in stunned silence. Thousands had been killed or wounded, and more thousands had been captured in the surrounding villages.

The council studied various plans, but all seemed inadequate to meet the emergency. As the meeting lengthened, a feeling of defeat filled the room. "We are helpless against so powerful an enemy," Ahaz said in despair. "How can we prevent ultimate surrender and slavery?"

A young nobleman who had been silent all evening now stood. Disapproving voices murmured at his action, for younger men were expected to be quiet in the presence of their elders. But the king motioned for silence. "None of you have produced a workable plan. Let him speak."

The youth bowed low at the king's recognition. "I hear that Tiglath-pileser, the king of Assyria, has entered Phoenicia, just north of Israel. Why not ask for his help?"

Several officials gasped at the thought of allying with the hated and bloodthirsty power. But Ahaz liked the suggestion. "What else can we do? We're lost if we don't get help."

Most heads reluctantly nodded in approval, although some questioned the wisdom of the idea. But the king had decided.

The last of the counselors still lingered in the outer hall when a clearly upset palace guard entered the king's chambers. He was leading a tall man dressed in sackcloth, with a leather belt around his waist. The king recognized Isaiah immediately. The man of God had surprised him in the fuller's field just after the news had arrived of the imminent invasion. The prophet had annoyed him then, and Ahaz felt even more impatient now.

"Is there no God in Judah that you send to pagans for aid?" Isaiah said before the king could stop him. "The hand you seek for salvation will stretch out to whip you. If you

22

will trust in Yahweh, He will save you from Israel and Syria." Then, before the king could order his removal, the prophet turned and strode away.

Recovering from his anger and disgust, Ahaz summoned three messengers and gave them two heavy bags of gold taken from the palace and Temple for the king of Assyria. "Go quickly," he barked. "All Judah depends on you."

The couriers left in the dark, easily slipping through the enemy lines. They had to hurry, or Jerusalem would be lost.

The following day Isaiah walked the streets of Jerusalem. "Calling on Assyria for help is dangerous," he proclaimed to those he met. "They will some day capture this city and enslave you. Why should Judah call on pagans when Yahweh is our Savior?" All day he preached his message in every part of the city. But the people would not listen.

The Assyrians accepted the invitation to intervene for Jerusalem. "Well," exclaimed the Assyrian cupbearer when he saw the gold sent by Ahaz, "if Judah can give that much to buy our help, they must have tremendous wealth."

"That's what I was thinking," King Tiglath-pileser commented. "Why don't we aid Judah, and then we can demand tribute?"

News quickly reached Jerusalem that Tiglath-pileser had allied with Ahaz. Israel and Syria quickly severed their treaty. They should have joined forces to fight Assyria, but instead each returned to protect his own land, and alone they were no match for the mighty Assyrian army.

Tiglath-pileser attacked Israel first, advancing down the valley of Esdraelon, capturing every city. But before he could besiege Samaria, assassins killed King Pekah and surrendered the nation. The Assyrians accepted Israel's choice of Hoshea as king when he promised to pay them taxes. Syria had no more success in fighting Tiglath-pileser than Israel. Even Damascus fell after a great slaughter.

Siege at the Gates

Quickly Tiglath-pileser set up his temporary headquarters in the ancient desert city and summoned his recent ally, Ahaz of Judah.

Ahaz took several members of his court with him, plus royal guards and several servants to carry the gold and other tribute. He dreaded his journey. The king had freely invited help from the world's most ruthless power, and that contrary to the counsel of Isaiah. Now he found himself enslaved, with no way out.

Tiglath-pileser was as brutal as he was powerful, and he seemed proud of his lack of mercy. The tyrant inflicted terrible tortures upon his captives. Deporting the people from a captured nation, he would resettle them in several different countries. Then he would repopulate their native land with captives from still other conquered areas. Usually this action would break the spirit of most nations, making rebellion more difficult.

Quickly Ahaz learned the meaning of servitude. He had to pay exorbitant yearly taxes to Assyria and he began to worship their god, Ashur. Such worship was considered a demonstration of loyalty. But sacrifice to Ashur in Tiglath-pileser's presence was only a beginning. Ahaz built an altar in the Temple of Yahweh and used it regularly to worship the pagan deity. The king agreed to every part of the treaty, even permitting Assyrian officials to accompany him to Jerusalem to see that he did it all.

Ahaz transformed the Temple into a pagan shrine, moving Yahweh's altar of burnt offering to the north side of the Temple court and erecting Ashur's altar in its place. Then the Judahite monarch himself offered sacrifices and commanded that all daily sacrifices be made on the altar of Ashur. Renouncing the worship of Yahweh, he zealously restored all the pagan high places. He seemed bent on destroying every remnant of the worship of the Creator.

Hezekiah could not understand what had come over his father. "Why does he stop worshipping Yahweh to sacrifice to foreign gods?" he asked his mother. "And why has he made Judah a slave to Assyria?" But she had no answer. Both consoled themselves that Ahaz had not forced them to participate in any of the rites. "Perhaps Father knows how we feel," the prince continued. "Perhaps he wants to spare us the terrible ordeal. But why does Father do it?"

Maybe Isaiah could explain what was going on, Hezekiah thought later. The prince hurried through the crowded streets to the prophet's humble home. He had often gone there. Sometimes Hezekiah had made the trip in the dark. The boy wished it were night now, as he felt the glare of hundreds of curious eyes . . . eyes that stared at him, the crown prince, whose destination, they knew, was the house of Yahweh's prophet. The door opened instantly to the boy's knock, and Hezekiah slipped inside with a sigh of relief. Isaiah would soothe the turmoil that stirred inside him.

"Your father has sinned," the prophet said, without apology. Grief and emotion filled his voice, and tears wet his eyes. "Judah will suffer because of Ahaz's folly. But you, Hezekiah, must be faithful to Yahweh. Someday you will become king. Then you can undo the great harm that your father has caused." He embraced the sobbing boy. "Hezekiah, you must dedicate yourself to Yahweh as never before."

Both prophet and prince remained silent for many moments, each absorbed in his own thoughts. But a loud knocking on the door startled them. Isaiah crossed the room and opened the rough plank door. A palace guard stood there, nervously toying with the handle of his sword. His face seemed pale, and he choked on his message. "The king wants Hezekiah to join the royal family in the valley of Hinnom."

As Isaiah stepped aside to allow the boy to exit, he whispered, "Be brave, Hezekiah. Yahweh will give you strength." The prince looked pleadingly into the prophet's eyes. No other words passed between them, but each knew the other's thoughts. They made an unspoken covenant of faithfulness to their Creator.

The royal family was already present when Hezekiah arrived. Abijah stood with the king's wives and concubines, each with their children beside them. Ahaz waited by himself near the pagan high place dedicated to Milcom, a god of the Ammonites.

Hezekiah noticed that Abijah cradled his little brother in her arms. The baby cooed happily as the mother cuddled him and caressed his head with her hand. Their mother wept softly, and the prince wondered why. As he embraced her with one arm to comfort her he realized that he had never seen such horror in her eyes. What could be the matter? His mind screamed, *Why have we been summoned here?*

But he didn't have long to wonder. Footsteps approached from behind, and he whirled around. The lad gazed full into his father's face. The king's wild eyes made Hezekiah feel as if he had never known the man before. Could this insane person be his father? His mind could not comprehend the nightmare he now found himself in.

When the king snatched at the infant, Abijah resisted. Ahaz then struck her in the face, and she collapsed to the ground. Seizing the child in his awkward hands, the king hurried toward the fire blazing in the Moloch tophet—the fire pit—of Milcom. Hezekiah's heart leaped into his throat. Only faintly did he hear his mother stumble to her feet and run toward the city, wailing hopelessly. His whole attention focused on his father about to lay his baby brother on those flames . . . to offer him to a pagan idol! How could it be? His mind whirled. *Why doesn't somebody stop him?*

Unable to control himself any longer, Hezekiah leaped toward his father, whose hands even now prepared to hurl the infant into the fire. The prince would save his brother, snatch him from the flames . . . from the madness of his father! But strong hands grasped the boy's arms, halting his flight in midair. A guard struggled to subdue him, lost his footing, and stumbled to the ground. The baby's cries of agony shattered the air. Hezekiah covered his ears and buried his face in the guard's tunic. But the screams of the burning child quickly ceased, and no one could help him now.

The king remained on his face before the tophet, praying to the pagan deity. The women and children numbly stared in various directions, their faces etched in horror. The guards fought their nausea after witnessing the sight. And Hezekiah, through hysterical sobs, prayed that Yahweh would end the madness . . . the horror of apostasy.

Chapter 3

A Boy Becomes King

The nightmare of his brother's death haunted Hezekiah for weeks. How could he ever forget his mother's frenzied sobs, and his own horror as the child perished in the flames? And how could he ever forgive his father? Perhaps he might forgive in time, but he would no longer respect the man whom others called their king, and he feared any contact with his father. Unable to control his anger, he simply avoided Ahaz.

The prince frequently visited Isaiah's humble home beside the city wall. The prophet knew of his ordeal, and he offered some much-needed fatherly counsel. They spent hours together, reading the Torah, discussing on the laws of Yahweh.

The boy would return from the prophet's home to console his mourning mother. Having lost her will to live, she remained in her chambers, refusing to see anyone except her closest friends and maidservants. But Hezekiah often brought her messages of promise from the Torah and the songs of David, as well as words of encouragement from the prophet. Weeks turned into months, but little by little the royal mother emerged from her mourning, and her smile once again shed warmth in the chill of the palace.

Ahaz only grew worse. He seemed bent on turning Judah against Yahweh. Not satisfied with constructing an altar to Ashur in the Temple court, the insane king now erected images and altars to Baal, Ashtoreth, Milcom, Marduk, and other pagan deities. And still not content, he built high places throughout the country for the convenience of the people.

One day the king realized that his son no longer tarried near the door of the audience chamber. Once the boy had listened as people brought their legal cases for the king's decision. It had delighted Ahaz that his son loved the royal duties so much, and he had looked forward to the time when the boy would judge Judah himself. But now he saw the prince only occasionally, and that at a great distance. *What is wrong?* he asked himself. *Why has the boy lost interest in the government?*

Finally Ahaz decided to speak to his son about it. Strolling in the royal gardens one evening, the king spotted Hezekiah out of the corner of his eye. The boy was trying to reach his chambers without attracting his father's attention, but the monarch seized the opportunity. "Hezekiah," he called. "Come here, my son."

The prince halted, his heart racing and his palms perspiring. Fearing the worst, he silently pleaded to God for aid. Then slowly he faced his father. The king's eyes seemed to have softened. *Perhaps I have nothing to fear,* Hezekiah consoled himself. *Maybe Father plans to repent and return to Yahweh.*

Ahaz's voice interrupted his thoughts. "Have you lost interest in the affairs at court, my son?" As Hezekiah relaxed, his father continued, "You enjoyed it before. What has happened?"

No longer could the prince avoid the issue. He must reveal how he felt. "Father"—the boy's voice quivered—"I have not come to court because of what you have done." The king recoiled, but Hezekiah went on. "First you made Judah a slave to Assyria. Then you erected an altar to Ashur in the Temple. I thought you had lost your reason. 'Surely,' I told myself, 'Father must know that Yahweh curses all who worship false gods.' And yet you worship foreign idols daily."

The king's face blanched, but Hezekiah hadn't finished. "You've turned your back on Yahweh, and even though the people follow you, they no longer respect you."

At last Ahaz found his voice. "But, my son," he whined, "I had to do all these things to prevent war with Assyria."

"Has Yahweh no power to save?" Hezekiah exploded. "And did the Assyrian king command you to sacrifice my brother?" The prince screamed the words. "No! You wanted to impress that horsefly from Assyria that you had really broken with Yahweh. So you murdered my brother to make yourself look good in his eyes!" The boy could speak no more. His body trembled with rage, and tears cascaded down his cheeks. Slowly he sank to his knees.

For the first time in his life, Ahaz found himself weeping. His voice was little more than a whisper. "Son, I know I have sinned much more than I ever dreamed possible. Why was I so foolish? How can Yahweh forgive me?"

Now the king began to pace the garden. After what seemed an eternity, he paused before the prince. "You speak the truth, my son. You have been more just than I have been to you and your mother. If only I could turn back," he began to wail. "If only I could have another chance! But it's too late. I'm a lost man!" His voice trailed off into a moan.

Hezekiah had never seen him like this. "But, Father," he urged, "Yahweh will forgive you if you turn from your sins."

But Ahaz did not seem to hear, and he staggered to his royal bedchamber. The prince remained in the garden until long after dark, trying to understand what had happened.

The sun peeped over the Mount of Olives as a servant left the king's sleeping chamber with a message for the Temple gatekeeper. Torn between conscience and his promises to Tiglath-pileser, Ahaz decided to close the Temple. "It's only a compromise," he told himself. "If I remove the altar of Ashur, Assyria will certainly attack me. Yet if the people continue to worship foreign deities in Yahweh's Temple, God will curse me."

A Boy Becomes King

Weeks passed, and Ahaz refused to see anyone. He turned the judgment of legal matters and other affairs of state over to his advisers. The nation went about its business, but the king became a recluse. Some days he would not even leave his bedroom or eat. Guilt weighed him down. And yet he spurned the only help offered—the counsel of Isaiah.

Hezekiah's twelfth birthday arrived, and the ceremonies proclaimed that the boy was now a man. But the joy seemed to go out of the occasion, for the king didn't attend. He still remained a recluse in his private chambers.

Late in the day a messenger arrived from the royal palace. Ahaz desired the prince's presence. That was all . . . no sign of what his father wanted . . . just a summons.

Leaving his guests, the prince approached his father's chambers, hardly prepared for the scene that greeted him. The monarch wore only his nightshirt . . . no royal robes . . . no jeweled crown . . . no golden scepter to welcome his well-dressed, princely son . . . not even a royal attendant to announce his arrival. The young man saw only a disheveled, drunken man sprawled on his ornate bed.

Ahaz motioned his son to a stool. His voice lifeless, the man seemed to have aged years since the day they had last met in the garden just a few weeks before. For a long moment neither uttered a word, but at last the ruler spoke. "My son," he began, his voice barely audible, "I cannot continue like this. I am no longer worthy to bear the title 'King of Judah.'" Ahaz paused as if to catch his breath, and then he continued, "I plan to anoint you as king of Judah, to co-rule with me. You are wise, my son. You will do far more for Judah than I have ever done." His hands trembled violently, and he bit his lip to keep his composure. "Will you accept my proposal?"

Although Hezekiah seemed young, the maturity in his eyes betrayed a man beneath the boyish face. "I will accept your proposal on one condition, Father." The king raised his eyebrows, but the lad went on, "I will reign with you, only if you give me full control of religion in the kingdom. You must let me lead our people back to Yahweh."

The monarch's lips curled into a slight smile. "I expected you to say that, yes. And I am sure you will do just that. But you must also promise me one thing." He paused, glancing through the window at the moon rising over the Mount of Olives. "Promise me you will continue paying tribute to Assyria as long as I live. That way you will prevent war with that mighty empire."

The prince quickly agreed to the condition. "As long as you are alive. But one day I will free Judah from Assyrian power."

For the first time in months Ahaz smiled. "Tell no one of our plans," he cautioned. "Go back to your feast now, and I will arrange for the coronation."

Spontaneously the prince broke into song as he returned to the banquet hall. *I will be king in a few days.* His mind reeled at the thought. *And then I will lead Judah back to Yahweh. O Lord,* he prayed, *make me the best king Judah ever had.*

The days flew by as Hezekiah prepared for his coronation. He told no one, and yet everyone knew. The whole nation seemed delighted, for they all adored the crown prince.

Coronation day arrived, and since the Temple was officially closed, the ceremony took place in the palace garden. Multitudes crowded the enclosure to witness the event. Isaiah and his family were there, and of course Abijah, the queen mother. "I hope you can always be as happy as you are today," Hezekiah whispered to her.

As the crown prince approached the garden, his eyes swept the scene before him. He abruptly stopped as he spotted the throne upon which he would sit. Was it by accident that it stood upon the very spot where he had accused his father of apostasy? Or had his father purposely erected it there to appease his nagging conscience?

The ceremony was shorter than that through which Ahaz had passed just a few years before. Hezekiah realized that the king had no desire to expose himself to public view any longer than necessary. In fact, the palace steward had told him that morning that his father planned to retire as soon as the coronation ended. The royal caravan already waited to transport King Ahaz and his family to the royal retreat in Lachish. Ahaz obviously meant to keep his promises.

The ceremony concluded, and the new sovereign headed for the royal banquet hall, surrounded by hundreds of the nation's greatest. Several hours passed before he realized that Ahaz had not come. "Where is my father?" he asked the steward.

"The king has already left for Lachish," the man replied. "He has taken all his wives and concubines, except Abijah."

"My mother is staying?"

"Yes, your majesty. King Ahaz wanted her to be here, as he said, 'to look after her son.' Your father also gave me one more order before he left."

"What was that?"

"All the servants are to follow your desires, King Hezekiah."

Now Hezekiah knew that his father would not interfere. He pitied the man. Sin had led him to the edge of insanity, and now, though only a young man, he appeared on the edge of the grave. But Hezekiah had little time to mourn his father. The new king had plans of his own for the future.

Late in the day following the coronation, Hezekiah summoned the high priest and his men. "Open the Temple again," he told them. "We have sinned by stopping the sacrifices and worshipping idols of gold, silver, and brass." The aged priests and the Levites marveled at the young man's maturity. They knew him to be a mere boy, and yet he acted and spoke as though he were a man of long experience.

The high priest stepped forward and bowed. "Your majesty," he said warmly, "you know that the Temple has been made impure by the idols and pagan altars. According to the laws of Moses, the Temple must be cleansed before we can use it again for the worship of Yahweh."

"Certainly we want to follow the Torah," Hezekiah agreed. "But we must start right away. Let us cleanse the Temple as soon as we can." The priest smiled at the youthful king's persistence, but the young man had more to say. "I will give you authority to work. Call all the priests and Levites together tomorrow morning. I will instruct them myself."

As the Temple staff left the court, a palace servant slipped through a back entrance and hurried to the house of the Assyrian legate. The servant knocked, and an irritated, paunchy ambassador met him. Hoping that no one had seen him, the servant tremblingly entered, and his story tumbled out: "The king plans to cleanse the Temple . . . to remove all pagan shrines, including Ashur's altar . . . to return Yahweh's altar to its rightful place."

The Assyrian scowled. "Sounds like treason to me. I'd better go see that boy-king at once."

Placing a piece of silver into the outstretched hand of the servant, the legate stepped into the waning day. Passing through the royal garden, where the king had been crowned the day before, the Assyrian strutted into the royal audience chamber. The herald announced him immediately, and he found himself standing before the boy monarch almost before he was ready to speak. Hezekiah's politeness unnerved him. His attitude certainly didn't appear rebellious.

The ambassador hesitated. Choosing his words carefully, he said, "Word has reached me of plans to reopen your nation's Temple."

"You have heard correctly," Hezekiah replied.

"I'm most thankful for that. I've been unable to burn incense to Ashur for some time now."

Hezekiah's smile disappeared. "We do not hesitate to tell you that we will clear Yahweh's Temple of all foreign idols."

The legate struggled to conceal his anger. "Surely you know that some will interpret your action as an act of treason."

"Yes, I know," the king answered politely. "I also know that Yahweh will not let any nation destroy Judah's worship. We will cleanse the Temple in spite of any outside threats." As the Assyrian official trembled in rage, Hezekiah added, "I know you must report this to your king. But get this straight—Judah has not rebelled. In fact, my servants will accompany you to Assyria to deliver the tribute. And I will continue to send it. But Judah will not worship foreign gods!"

The Assyrian legate, his slaves, and several of Hezekiah's servants began their journey at dawn. As the group passed through East Street and by the Temple gates they could see that many priests and Levites had already gathered there.

Just before leaving the city, the official paused to look at the crowd in front of the Temple. He spat on the ground in contempt, his voice barely audible except to a servant standing beside him. "Tiglath-pileser will have Hezekiah's head for this." Then spurring his horse, he disappeared down into the Kidron Valley.

Chapter 4

A Nation Returns to God

The sun had been visible for only a few minutes, and already Jerusalem stirred with excitement. Men and children gathered in small groups everywhere. Women hurried to fetch water from the spring outside the city gate so they could return in time to hear the king.

Many people liked the religious reform, and they rejoiced that their boy-king had reopened the Temple. The closing of the sacred house had hurt the Levites most, for their whole lives centered around its services. Now they could serve Yahweh once again.

But the revival angered some of the priests. They had become wealthy on the apostasy. Instead of teaching the law of Moses in the Temple precincts, they had obtained positions as tutors and chaplains to the wealthy. Now they didn't want to lose their good-paying positions. Hezekiah's reformation would put them back to teaching the Scriptures with no pay except a Temple allowance.

"For years," Isaiah told Hezekiah, "I have urged this nation to repent. Now, at last, the people are responding." The prophet continued to encourage the king to restore the Temple. "Don't listen to the warnings of those who say Assyria will punish Judah. Yahweh has promised to protect us."

Everybody in Jerusalem seemed to have gathered in East Street. Their excited voices reverberated against the stone and plastered walls. But as the herald announced the approach of the king, all eyes turned toward the palace, straining to see him.

Hezekiah appeared tall for his age, and the crowds fell back to make way. Shouts of "Long live the king!" rang out, at first here and there, but then the chants blended as though rising from a single voice: "Long live the king! Long live the king!"

The noise became deafening. Hezekiah's knees felt weak, and his hands trembled as he glanced at the seething multitudes. With a silent prayer for wisdom, he straightened his shoulders and held his head erect as he climbed the steps in front of the Temple and turned to face the masses.

The chant grew as Hezekiah smiled. When he raised his scepter, the noise slowly died. All became hushed except for the occasional bark of a dog on some neighboring street. The breeze fluttered the leaves of the locust tree that stood beside the Temple gate and gently stirred the folds of the king's robes.

"People, listen to me." Hezekiah noticed that even the children paid attention to his words. "Sanctify yourselves and consecrate the Temple of Yahweh. Your ancestors have been unfaithful to Him, turning their faces away from the place that Yahweh has made His home. They closed the doors of the Temple, extinguished the sacred lamps, and offered no incense or burnt offerings. So God's anger has fallen on Judah and on Jerusalem. He has made us an object of derisive whistling. This is why our fathers have fallen by the sword, and our sons, daughters, and wives have been taken captive.

"I am determined to make peace with Yahweh so that His fierce anger will turn away from us. My people, Yahweh has chosen you to serve Him. He wants you to conduct His worship and to offer incense to Him."

After the king had finished, the city's inhabitants remained silent for a long moment. Then suddenly a Levite shouted, "Amen!" and soon a chorus of Amens sounded from every side.

Hezekiah rejoiced that they had accepted his appeal. Turning to the Temple gate, he opened the latch and pushed on the heavy door. One of the guards slipped to his side and added his weight to the effort. The door swung inward, and after crossing the outer court, the king and his servants soon gazed into the sacred court.

Necks stretched, and people tried to push toward the front of the crowd, seeking to see better. They gasped at the trash littering the court. In the center, where Yahweh's altar of burnt offerings should have been, huddled the altar of Ashur. Yahweh's altar rested against the northern wall, half-covered with debris.

On the Temple steps and elsewhere sat images of Milcom, Ashur, Marduk, and others along with their altars and other cult objects. Around each image one could see the burnt remains of sacrifices offered to pagan gods.

After a long silence the Levites organized themselves into teams and began carting the idols, the ashes and bone fragments, and Ashur's altar down to the Kidron Valley landfill. Everyone seemed surprised that so much trash had accumulated through the years. It took the Levites eight days to carry all of it to the city dump and to scrub and polish the Temple court with all its sacred utensils. And it required another eight days for the priests to clean out the Temple. But finally it was ready for the daily services.

Hezekiah came personally to inspect it. "You have worked hard," he praised the men. "Yahweh has inspired you. Now, spread the word: The daily services begin tomorrow."

"Amen!" they responded in chorus.

The Temple court loomed dark in the predawn stillness. Here and there, light flickered from the torches carried by the priests and Levites arriving early to prepare for the morning sacrifice. Excitement vibrated in the air as Temple officials verified that every vessel was in its proper place. Newly appointed musicians inspected the cymbals, psalteries, harps, and ram's-horn trumpets to assure that everything was ready.

People filtered into the outer court, drifting to secluded corners to stand or bow in prayer. Levites led animals from the Temple stables into the inner court and tied them in place.

The spreading light of dawn washed the shadows away, and the scattered groups expanded into crowds. By the time the rising sun peeped over the brow of the Mount of Olives, people overflowed into East Street. The king and his nobles had difficulty reaching their reserved places at the doorway of the inner court.

The high priest and his helpers began their work. The sacrifices offered that morning benefited all Israel. Those who desired to confess their sins to Yahweh could accept both the morning and the evening sacrifices as an atonement for their transgressions. The priests usually slew one lamb each morning, and one each evening. But today they presented several offerings to atone for the terrible sin of defiling the Temple of Yahweh.

The priests killed and skinned the animals one by one as musicians and singers performed the psalms of David. The smell of burning flesh filled the air, and songs of praise mingled with the ascending smoke and incense.

The Temple officials sacrificed seven bullocks, seven rams, seven lambs, and seven male goats. The priests slew, bled, skinned, and quartered each animal. They burned much of each animal upon the altar, but reserved the blood to sprinkle some of it on the altar, and then took some into the holy place to dab upon the horns of the golden altar of incense. This symbolized the transfer of the people's confessed sins to the Temple.

Finally the last animal had been slain, the final blood spattered, and the whiffs of smoke ascended forever into the heavens. The people bowed with their faces to the ground, pleading for God's mercy. Then, as they arose from their prostrate positions, they saw Hezekiah standing before them. "Praise be to Yahweh of hosts," he proclaimed, "for He has heard our prayers and has returned to us." With deep emotion, he appealed to his people: "Repent of your sins and return to Yahweh your God." Briefly he explained the meaning of the sin offerings required by the Scriptures and called for them to bring their tithes and thank offerings to God as well.

Slowly the people departed, loathe to leave the sacred presence of Yahweh. But the courtyard remained active all day with worshippers arriving with their sin offerings and tithes for Yahweh. The 70 bullocks, 100 rams, and 200 lambs they offered were far more than a few priests could handle by themselves. So the Levites helped to skin and prepare the animals for sacrifice. Besides burnt offerings, the people contributed 600 oxen and 3,000 sheep as tithes and offerings.

The sun descended behind Mount Zion, and twilight clothed the city in blue-gray as Isaiah entered the royal court. "Welcome, my good friend," Hezekiah greeted him. "Sit here at my right hand, for you deserve the honor."

"Yahweh has accepted His people once more," rejoiced the man of God. "But morning and evening sacrifices are only a beginning. We must start Passover again." Briefly Isaiah outlined the history and procedure of the festival. "Passover marks the deliverance of Israel's firstborn from the hand of the angel of death at the Exodus," he explained. "It's usually held on the fourteenth day of the first month each year."

"But that's already passed!" Hezekiah exclaimed.

"Yes, my son. But the law says that anyone who is unable to eat the Passover in the first month because of uncleanness can do it on the fourteenth day of the second month."

"I see."

"This provision fits the entire nation now." Isaiah's face beamed. "So we can have the feast on the fourteenth day of next month."

"That's wonderful," Hezekiah agreed. "And why don't we invite Israel too?"

The two men discussed the idea for some time, and soon the palace vibrated with excitement as scribes scurried toward the court.

At sunrise the royal stables stirred as grooms saddled every mount for the royal messengers. And none too soon. Almost immediately men darted from the king's presence with their scrolls safely tucked into leather pouches. Mounting their steeds, they rode out through the palace gate, down the narrow streets, and through city gates that opened in every direction. Curious crowds wondered why the king had sent so many messengers. "Does an enemy threaten to besiege the city?" several asked. "Does the king need an army?"

At last a messenger came to the palace gate and motioned for silence. Everyone listened to catch each word. The man unrolled a scroll and read it in a high-pitched, monotonous voice:

"Sons of Israel, come back to Yahweh, and He will return to you. Do not be like your fathers and brothers who were unfaithful to Yahweh and whom He handed over to destruction. Do not be stubborn now, but yield to Yahweh and come to His sanctuary. If you serve Yahweh, He will turn His anger from you. Your brothers and your sons will win favor with their conquerors and will return to this land. If you return to Him, He will not turn His face from you. Come now, and join with us in the Passover on the fourteenth day of the second month."

The messenger rolled the scroll up again, and the people stood silently for a minute. Then someone shouted, "Allelujah!" and several replied, "Amen!" They scattered to tell friends and neighbors of the king's message. "Yahweh has blessed His people," they shouted. "We're having the Passover next month."

But the messengers who traveled northward into the kingdom of Israel encountered a different reception. Israel had lived without the Temple for 200 years. Most of the people no longer believed in Yahweh, but referred to Him as the God of Judah. They laughed at the invitation to celebrate Passover. "Why would we want to worship Yahweh?" they mocked. "We are more enlightened than our ancestors. Now we worship the gods of the land—Baal, Ashtoreth, Milcom, and Ashur."

Hoshea, king of Israel, angrily ordered his soldiers to drive the messengers away. But his counselors urged caution. "Assyria may consider military action of this kind as rebellion against them."

"That's right," another suggested. "And we need every soldier here at home to protect Samaria."

A few Israelites, however, realized that Hezekiah spoke the truth. "We should return to Yahweh," one man said to his wife. "Let's go to Jerusalem for the Passover." A scattering from Asher, Manasseh, Zebulun, and Issachar did appear among the multitudes in the Temple. But only a few.

Jerusalem overflowed as Passover approached. Many had to camp outside the walls, for no space remained within the city. And many pilgrims loathed the pagan altars still remaining in and around Jerusalem. They tumbled the shrines into the dust, carting them off to the Kidron Valley dumping grounds. Thus the people prepared their hearts and their city for Passover.

On the fourteenth day of the second month, at the time of the evening sacrifice, the people killed the Passover lamb in every dwelling. Each family roasted the lamb whole and ate it. Many, however, had failed to sanctify themselves for the feast and discovered that they were not allowed to slay the lamb. Levites had to help them. But even then, some came to Hezekiah and asked, "Is it proper for us to eat the Passover when we are ceremonially unclean?"

"I don't know," the king replied. "Let me ask Isaiah." He soon returned with a smile. "Go ahead and eat, for God will forgive your transgressions."

The feast of unleavened bread lasted seven days following Passover. During this time the people attended the morning and evening services, and Levites traveled from one camp to another teaching the laws of Moses.

Hezekiah personally mingled with the people, encouraging them to yield their lives to Yahweh. Though only a lad of 13, he yet seemed mature beyond his years in his thoughts and actions.

The feast ended all too soon, and the people requested the king to extend it. So Hezekiah added another week. It stood out as the greatest Passover since Solomon—and the last many Israelites would ever know. Soon—unknown to any of them—the Assyrians would deport the inhabitants of the northern kingdom.

"I charge you to live faithfully for Yahweh," Hezekiah said on the last day of the feast. "Refrain from your old ways. Serve the Lord, and He will bless you all. When you return to your villages," he advised, "destroy every idol, every altar, every high place."

The crowds dispersed, a new fervor filling their hearts. They determined to follow Hezekiah' s counsel. Bands traveled throughout Judah and into Israel removing pagan shrines. Hezekiah even destroyed the Nehushtan—the bronze serpent that Moses had made in the wilderness—because the people had begun worshiping it instead of the God it represented.

Priests and Levites organized themselves so that they

43

could continue the Temple services. They established scribal schools to teach reading, writing, and the laws of Moses. And they began to copy scrolls to make the Scriptures more available throughout the land. The people faithfully brought their tithes and offerings. All the Temple storerooms overflowed by the end of the seventh month.

Chapter 5

The Death of Israel

Three years had passed since the Temple reform, and Hezekiah continued to send annual tribute to Assyria. Tiglath-pileser had been furious at the news of the purge of pagan religion. "Hezekiah rebels against me," he roared at the Judahite ambassadors. "He won't get away with it. I'll attack him within the year!"

But he had needed his armies elsewhere to squash larger rebellions. And alas, he died before the year ended.

His son Shalmaneser V, though not as strong as his father, was still a skilled military leader. He intended to carry out his father's wish to destroy the "rebellion" in Judah. But troubles had plagued him, too, and he was unable to punish Judah.

Meanwhile, 15-year-old Hezekiah prepared his country for certain Assyrian invasion. The city teemed with people actively strengthening the defenses of Jerusalem. The metalworkers pounded their anvils from dawn until dusk, fashioning bronze spearheads, swords, and other weapons for the king's army. Storehouses overflowed with grain. To prevent spoilage, the city's inhabitants stored grain in earthenware jars and sealed them with a lid after they had inspected the contents. The seal protected the grain from moisture and rodents. Other warehouses became arsenals for weapons —crammed with bows, thousands of arrows, spears, sling stones, and other military equipment.

Jerusalem had no spring within its walls, and the city had to store water in large rock cisterns for the long months of a siege. So women, forming endless lines, transported water from the springs outside the city to fill the many cisterns.

Even the children helped. Girls carried smaller jars. Boys ran errands, hauled finished weapons from the metal shops to the king's arsenals, and assisted farmers in unloading grain at the storehouses.

People in the country around the city sold produce or donated material for the city's defense. More farmers than usual were in the city now, all eager to make lodging arrangements for their families. Should the Assyrians attack, no one wanted to be caught outside the city.

Daily the army drilled in the valleys and on the hills around the city. Soldiers continually marched on the walls, practicing maneuvers so that they could quickly move from one place to another. Defending Jerusalem would be no easy task. Though far smaller than the mighty cities of Babylon and Nineveh—whose walls extended for many miles around each city—Jerusalem was still the largest city in Palestine, covering 86 acres. In contrast, the city of Samaria had an area of only 19 acres.

The general fear in Judah intensified when the kingdom of Israel openly defied Assyria. It also had stopped paying tribute and even expelled the Assyrian ambassador from Samaria. Invasion from Assyria seemed even more imminent when Israel allied forces with Syria, Gaza, Hamath, and several other small nations. They combined their armies and sent envoys to Egypt seeking military aid. Jerusalem became even more on edge when Israel's ambassadors called on Hezekiah, requesting that Judah join them—only six years since their own attack on Judah.

As the envoys settled in the palace, awaiting an audience, King Ahaz returned from his exile at Lachish. He wanted to observe how his son prepared for a siege. Ahaz inspected the storehouses, the cisterns, the armory, and noticed that the

Temple was open again, which brought a frown to his face. When he learned that envoys from Israel were in the city, he vowed to stop the trouble before it started.

Hezekiah knew nothing of his father's presence in the city. The old king had disguised himself, and most failed to recognize him. Therefore it somewhat shocked Hezekiah when his father strode into his audience chamber, interrupting a conversation with Isaiah. The prophet excused himself and left.

Having not forgotten the murder of his brother, and blaming much of the Assyrian troubles on the fact that Ahaz had forsaken Yahweh, Hezekiah felt uncomfortable in his father's presence. But he decided to bury the past.

"How are you, my son?" Ahaz greeted Hezekiah warmly. "I'm pleased to find Jerusalem so well prepared. But, son, could we discuss the ambassadors from Israel?" Ahaz tried to imply that he would not interfere, yet he wanted his son to realize that he still possessed authority.

Hoping Ahaz would not reassert himself, Hezekiah took the lead and revealed his plans. "Father, I have already decided to reject Israel's offer."

"Wonderful!" Ahaz smiled. "I hoped you would be wise enough to recognize trouble." Then the father once again reminded his son of their agreement to continue the Assyrian tribute.

"Yes, Father. I have kept my word. And meanwhile I'm building Judah's strength so that one day we can be free."

Ahaz refrained from any mention of the Temple, and Hezekiah noticed the omission. "Father, I have prayed that Yahweh will guard His people, and Isaiah assures me that He will. I have done all I can to protect the city myself. Now I must wait for Yahweh to work, and I firmly believe He will."

Although Ahaz nodded at Hezekiah's expression of faith, he otherwise ignored it. He knew that his son had spoken openly of Yahweh for his sake. "You're right, of course, my son. But I have gone too far to ever return to Yahweh."

Something in the way he said it caused Hezekiah to realize that he really meant it. So the younger man changed the subject. "The Israelite ambassadors will arrive in just a few minutes. Would you join me while I reveal my decision?"

The older monarch glanced at the water clock sitting in the corner of the room. The large cone-shaped jar was filled with water that seeped through a pin-sized hole in the bottom. A person could read the time by the level of the water against marks on the side of the jar. It was the seventh hour since sunrise. The father wondered at Hezekiah's trust in inviting him to such an important conference. "Yes, my son," he answered. "Of course . . . I will be honored to join you."

Nearly an hour passed before Ahaz rejoined Hezekiah. He now appeared every bit the king he really was. The two monarchs seated themselves on a dual throne, and a herald announced the envoys.

Hezekiah smiled to see the astonished Israelites' faces when they recognized his father. They wouldn't take it as a friendly omen, he mused to himself. They knew how their former king had fought against Ahaz.

Although the two rulers sat side by side, the son actually held out the royal scepter to the ambassadors. "My government cannot help Israel now." Hezekiah was courteous but firm, while Ahaz remained silent. "Please express my regrets to King Hoshea."

Everyone—from chamberlain to door servants—knew that something important had occurred. Two kings—father and son—occupied the throne, but the father openly permitted his son to speak for the kingdom. Obviously Hezekiah was stronger than Ahaz, or it would never have happened.

Ahaz recognized it more than anyone else. He was finished as king. While the wisdom of his son pleased him, it still hurt to assume second place in public. Never again, he decided, would he interfere with Hezekiah's government. Though he lived another 10 years, he would never again appear in public.

The ambassadors from Israel had been gone but a few weeks when Shalmaneser V marched toward Palestine to destroy the conspiracy. Hezekiah realized that when Shalmaneser finished in the north, he could well advance on Judah.

News arrived daily from the north . . . tales of woe as city after city fell. Damascus, Hamath, Gaza, and hundreds of smaller towns crumbled as thousands died and the conquering armies deported tens of thousands more.

The people of Judah craved news of Israel most. The two kingdoms had split 200 years before and had often fought each other. Yet they were still descendants of Jacob. They inwardly desired to help each other in a crisis. When Shalmaneser attacked Hoshea's army, some in Jerusalem wanted to rush to the aid of their kindred, but Hezekiah said no. Their help would soon be needed at home.

Israel's army disintegrated in hours. Assyria's Elamite archers were deadly accurate, and the light armor of the infantry allowed them an easy victory over the poorly armed Israelites. The Assyrian cavalry was impossible to stop.

Israelite corpses carpeted the battlefield, and the remnants fled in a thousand directions. By day's end the invaders had Hoshea bound, riding on a bouncing oxcart, headed for Nineveh and imprisonment. Judah feared that Jerusalem would be next, but they misjudged the Assyrian mind. Its armies had captured Israel's king, but Shalmaneser would not quit until he held Samaria, the capital. Some of the Assyrian forces besieged Samaria, while others raided every small town in Israel. They destroyed countless villages and killed or deported the people.

Samaria, though small, had thick walls. The people had

stocked food and water for more than a year. With well-trained defenders, the city could easily hold the Assyrians at bay. Months went by, but the Assyrians remained. No one could escape from Samaria. When food and water began to fail, the once haughty people realized that their days were numbered unless the Assyrians tired first.

For more than two years Shalmaneser continued the siege, until Samaria's food, water, and hope had disappeared and the people perished from starvation and constant disease. Some killed and ate their own children. But at last they could hold out no longer.

Unknown to the Samaritans, Shalmaneser had died during the final months of the siege. Sargon II, one of his generals, promptly galloped off to Nineveh to seize the throne, but the army stayed behind to finish the siege. Finally Samaria's leaders surrendered, and Assyrians flooded the capital, taking everything of value and leveling the city. They executed many leaders and deported the rest of the people— 27,290 men, women, and children. Israel would never recover from the loss. The most talented of the people were gone—soldiers, officials, craftsmen, and merchants. Only a few unskilled and poorly organized farmers remained.

With the news of Samaria's fall, panic spread in Judah. Every tongue inquired of neighbor, friend, or official: "Will the Assyrians come here next?" Some feared it had been a mistake to cleanse the Temple and anger the pagan gods that had been worshiped there. Many spoke of repairing the altar of Ashur and replacing it in the Temple.

When talk of restoring the altar of Ashur reached Isaiah and Hezekiah, they summoned the leaders to meet them in the Temple court. But most of the city gathered also, grasping for some word of hope. The sight of their 18-year-old king, with his newly sprouting beard, began to reassure the people.

His voice had deepened since his first speech a few years

before. "I understand your feelings about the loss of our kins-people in Israel. And you fear the Assyrians will come here next. People, we must trust in Yahweh to save us."

Then Hezekiah hesitated, searching the thousands of faces to see their reactions. "Yahweh has blessed our nation since we purified His Temple. And He is still blessing us. Even now," his face broke into a huge grin, "word has reached us that the Assyrian army has returned to its own land."

Excited voices questioned the king's announcement.

"It is true," Hezekiah assured them. "Our scouts watched them march toward the north. Why should anyone speak of rebuilding the altar of Ashur? Has not Yahweh saved us from our enemies?" A murmur rolled through the crowd, but the king continued, "King Sargon of Assyria has taken his army to fight against Urartu, far to the north. I'm sure it will be months before he can return."

A cheer exploded from the crowd. When at last it subsided, Isaiah stepped forward to speak. "Our brother, Israel, has forsaken Yahweh, and Yahweh has forsaken him." The prophet glanced down at his sandals for a moment. "Yahweh made a covenant with Israel and gave them a command: 'You are not to worship alien gods. You are to worship only Yahweh, who brought you out of the land of Egypt. You are to observe His commandments, which He gave you in writing. Worship Yahweh alone, for He is your God, and He will deliver you out of the power of all your enemies.' But Israel would not listen.

"Remember that Hezekiah appealed to Israel to return to God. He invited the people to attend the Passover feast. Most refused, laughing at the messengers. But some came, repented of their sins, and still worship Yahweh. Even though they go to an alien land, they will be true to God. They will teach the pagans to worship Yahweh." Isaiah then pleaded with those assembled before the Temple to be faithful to their Creator. "He will protect and save all of us from the hated Assyrians."

It sobered the people to realize that they had been about to give up their faith when God was sending the Assyrians back home. Each heart vowed anew to be faithful to Yahweh.

Three years later the impoverished farmers in Israel rebelled. Once more they formed alliances with the surrounding nations. Again the Assyrian sword flashed in the land, again the soil became red with blood, again the sky darkened from the smoke of burning villages, and again streams of captive people tramping toward Assyrian exile choked the roads. Sargon completed the devastation this time, leaving nothing behind. And to make sure that the land would cause him no further trouble, he resettled the country with Arabs, Medes, and people from other conquered areas.

Israel was no more. Only Judah survived to teach the nations about Yahweh. But how long could it exist?

Chapter 6

Plans for Rebellion

Hezekiah struggled to build his country's power. No one knew when Sargon would arrive to punish Judah for threatening to sever its ties with Assyria.

Life in Judah drifted into the ancient pattern of the centuries, except for the daily military maneuvers. The countryside turned countless shades of green as farms and vineyards returned to full production. The city hummed with activity as each of its thousands of inhabitants conducted his or her personal business. Few people thought of the Assyrian overlords just a few days' journey north.

A visitor in Jerusalem would scarcely have suspected that the city had prepared for a siege. The bazaar crawled with people, and the streets overflowed with produce that spilled into the walkways. Loaded pack animals trudged through the throngs, coming or going from one shop to another, beginning or ending a tedious journey, taking goods to sell in some distant city or bringing rare items for sale in Jerusalem.

Farmers haggled over the prices of their produce. Competition was always keen, but a tolerant spirit dominated the marketplace. The Phoenician merchants, however, were somewhat less friendly. They had journeyed long distances to peddle their wares for a profit. Some lived in the city and had servants to operate their caravans. But many smaller merchants traveled the routes themselves—over the mountains to such seaports as Tyre, Sidon, and Joppa. Specializing in imports, they sold costly gems, exquisite cloth, gold and silver jewelry, rare spices, fine-grained woods, and exotic animals. As a group they bargained hard and less pleasantly than the local traders.

Jerusalem's industrial sections vibrated with activity. Smiths hammered their anvils and stoked their hearths, fashioning sickles, plowshares, and kitchen utensils. Potters spun on their wheels water pots, cooking pots, large and small dishes, and even an occasional water clock for a wealthy noble. The weavers manufactured fine yard goods for garments, coarse material for sacks and tents, and beautifully decorated rugs and tapestries for the wealthy.

The gold and silver artists tapped with their small mallets and engraved with their precision tools, producing jewelry of fine craftsmanship for the rich. They also made ornately decorated vessels for the palace or the Temple and various articles of usefulness and beauty for both home and foreign markets.

The local carpenters crafted furniture, plows, chairs, looms for the weavers, doors, gates for animal folds and city walls, bows and arrows, ornate staffs, and yokes for work animals. One could find anything made of wood in different stages of construction in one of the city's small carpenter shops.

Women busied themselves with tending the children and the endless tasks of the home. They baked the bread and fetched the water in large gallon-size clay pots carried on their heads (sometimes they had to walk a mile to reach the water, and the return trip was all uphill). Also the women cared for the animals with the help of older children.

Families kept their animals in pens attached to the houses, though the livestock more often stayed in stalls on the first floor of the house, while the family lived on the second floor.

Elderly men often gathered at the main city gate or at the Temple gate to act as judges. People brought their problems for the elders to settle. Disagreeing neighbors would summon witnesses so that the judges could make reliable decisions. But mostly the men chatted about local news or questioned travelers about foreign events.

Children, when they were not doing chores for their families, played games in the streets or courtyards. They enjoyed wrestling, boxing, and dancing to the beat of tambourines. In quieter moments they played games that resembled chess and cribbage.

By now Hezekiah had been married for several years. He also had a number of concubines, given to him by wealthy nobles of other nations. The secondary wives lived in a women's dormitory, except when summoned by the king. They were actually servants with specific work to do. Some helped in the kitchen while others wove cloth or made other needed material for the palace grounds. But they often assembled in the women's quarters to exchange gossip.

The king led a busy life. Foreign ambassadors frequently sought his advice, for he had gained a reputation as a wise and understanding ruler. Occasionally another country asked for an alliance against Assyria, but he refused to commit to any of them. He had promised that while Ahaz lived he would send the annual tribute to Assyria and refrain from rebelling against it.

Daily Hezekiah held court to settle the disagreements between people referred to him by the city elders. Such matters were usually the most difficult—cases beyond their ability to decide.

Now in his early 20s, Hezekiah was tall and with quick eyes and a ready mind. Little escaped his attention. His servants and advisers believed he had almost superhuman understanding. He always seemed to know what was happening in his kingdom.

Usually his decisions pleased the people. While his solutions were not always popular, most realized that they were right. The inhabitants of Judah could have confidence in a man who trusted God and accepted the counsel of Isaiah.

"We can never survive financially," Hezekiah asserted to his royal treasurer one day, "as long as we continue paying heavy tribute to Assyria. We've got to stop it sometime. We must have our freedom!"

"But you know what that means," the other man replied. "That means those murderous Assyrians will attack Judah."

"I know." Hezekiah felt his hands were tied. "I promised my father to pay as long as he lives." And the young king had kept his bargain. But he also prepared for the time when his father would no longer be around. "When that day comes," he explained, "I can stop the tribute payments."

"If you plan to do that," the treasurer warned, "you better build stronger defenses."

"Yes, you're right." The king studied the pattern of the wall designs for a minute. "We must be prepared to withstand the most devastating army ever to assemble And we can."

Secretly Hezekiah conferred with his advisers to plan for Jerusalem's safety.

"How can we guarantee the lives of our people during a siege by Assyria?" one of his generals asked. "How can Jerusalem survive the long months of an attack with no water source within the city walls?"

"The general is right," court recorder Joah broke in. "The minute Assyrians appear over the nearest mountain, our people will have to depend on the cisterns. From that moment, our days will be numbered by the amount of water in those cisterns, and the Assyrians know it. Look what happened to Samaria."

"That's all true." Hezekiah stood, leaning on the table before him and supporting his weight with both fists. "But I have an idea. It may seem far-fetched at first, but I think it may be within our reach." A smile crossed his face as the counselors leaned forward in suspense. "Why not tunnel water from the Gihon to some point within the walls?"

"Impossible!" Shebna, the steward, protested. "Why . . . Gihon is in the valley. Everyone knows that water can't run uphill!"

"That's true," Hezekiah persisted. "But the southern edge of Jerusalem near the king's gardens is lower than Gihon." His eyes narrowed in thought, and he stared out the window. "Why not tunnel the water to that spot?"

Mouths dropped open around the dimly lit room. "That's on the other side of the mountain," Joah objected, "almost a thousand cubits away! And everyone knows that Jerusalem stands on solid limestone."

The king unrolled a scroll. "I have presumed to draft some plans. It's not as impossible as it seems." To the counselors' amazement, the drawings showed every detail clearly.

"Well, I'll be," Shebna finally conceded. "It really looks feasible."

"It will be expensive and time-consuming," Joah put in, "but its advantages will outweigh the effort."

The council agreed that the project should begin. The king commissioned the royal engineers to prepare the final plans at once.

"Another matter needs to be settled," Hezekiah continued. "We must protect the roads that lead to Jerusalem against invaders. I think the highway most likely to be used by an advancing enemy is the one approaching from the southwest, by way of Lachish." On a map of Judah he stabbed his finger at the city of the royal retreat. "This little city commands a mountain pass, and I believe it is the key to Jerusalem's defense."

"The royal retreat is there," one of the generals observed. "The city already has strong walls and towers."

"That's right," Hezekiah agreed. "And they can be

strengthened and made impregnable to attack."

Just then a royal courier rushed into the room with an urgent dispatch. The king listened to the whispered message and paled.

"What is it, your majesty?" Joah asked.

The servant left, and Hezekiah sat motionless. His eyes focused into space, a look of surprise on his face. Finally he found his voice. "My father . . . Ahaz . . . died last night in Lachish." He wet his dry lips and slowly his color began to return. Drops of sweat beaded on his forehead. Without further word he hastened from the room.

The counselors were too stunned for words. Long after the king had departed, they stared at each other, fearful of expressing their thoughts. Perhaps but days would pass before they broke the bands of Assyria. The plans they had drafted today would soon be done. And perhaps quicker than any of them wished, the Assyrian armies would test their defenses.

Hezekiah hurried to his mother's quarters, questions plaguing his mind. *Has she heard?* he wondered. *Will she mourn? She was my father's main wife, yet she chose to stay with me in Jerusalem rather than be with him. Perhaps she simply couldn't bear to see his continual degeneration.*

Abijah had already learned the news, but instead of weeping, she simply sat gazing out the window. Quietly the two reviewed the older man's last years. "Ahaz grew weaker after he left Jerusalem," she said. "He was in his early forties when he died, and yet he looked much older." She paused for a time. "And he continued his idolatry in spite of your decree outlawing pagan worship in Judah."

"I thought the people destroyed every pagan altar!" Hezekiah replied in surprise.

"They did," his mother answered. "But Ahaz built a secret altar near Lachish. Idolatry and intemperance weakened his body and mind. He died of a disease common to old age."

Few attended the royal funeral. Hezekiah and his mother were there, as well as Ahaz's other wives and concubines. A number of the old king's trusted servants also came, plus some children and old men who watched out of curiosity. But few in Judah wanted to remember the man who had again led the nation into apostasy. To the average person, Ahaz passed unmourned.

Later in the day, as Hezekiah and Abijah sat alone in her house, she wept. "I don't miss him at all," she sobbed. "But I remember how strong and good he was when I married him, and how much I loved him then." She wiped the tears from her reddened eyes. "I remember how he drifted away from the Lord, from his people . . . and from me. He died yesterday," she said, "but we lost him years ago when he rebelled against Yahweh."

Neither mother nor son mentioned the terrifying scene in the Kidron Valley years before. But neither could prevent the memory from stabbing a wound afresh through the heart.

Finally Abijah broke the silence. "The thing that haunts me is his wasted life. He could have been such a strong and good king if only he had been faithful." She gazed at her handsome son for a moment, her eyes still moist from weeping. Slowly a smile caressed the corners of her lips.

Hezekiah studied his mother. She was nearly 40. Life had been terrible for her. Most people her age were old and weathered, yet she was still beautiful. He loved her far more than he realized.

Again her voice broke the stillness of the evening calm. "My life has been hard because of my husband's sins. But how glad I am that my son has not followed in his father's steps!" Tears flowed again—not now those of sorrow but of joy. "I will forget that I was ever the wife of Ahaz. Now I shall consider myself the mother of good king Hezekiah."

The king took his mother into his arms. Tears ran into his beard, and his voice cracked as he spoke. "By the grace of Yahweh, I will never disappoint you."

"By His grace, you won't . . . , my son."

Chapter 7

United They Fall

Dissatisfaction filled Jerusalem. Judah had paid tribute to Assyria for more than 20 years, draining the country of its wealth. Hezekiah sensed the mounting tension. "The people's nerves are near a breaking point," he confided to Shebna. "If we don't act quickly, they might rebel against my authority."

The king paced the floor as his steward waited by the door. "I've wanted rest from the Assyrians for years. But how can we escape? They have the world's most powerful army. Look at the other nations," he pointed into space. "The deserted ruins of their most prosperous cities look like so many tombs. If I rebel, it will mean certain suicide."

"And there are many opportunities," Shebna volunteered.

"There certainly are. Even now, ambassadors from Ashdod invite me to join them. It would be an odd alliance—Philistia, Moab, Edom, and Egypt. They're all enemies. At any other time they'd be tearing each other apart."

"These are strange times."

"And perilous," Hezekiah added. "Many countries are willing to bury the sword to unite against an unbeatable common foe."

"I'm sure Assyria's use of brutal tactics makes freedom that much more desirable, no matter who your allies are," the steward concluded.

"Exactly!" Hezekiah hesitated for a minute. "But if I join this alliance, I risk war with Assyria. That could mean the end of Judah. Thousands of our people would suffer torture, deportation, or death."

"But if we continue as slaves, you face national bankruptcy, internal strife, and perhaps the loss of your throne—if not your very life."

"I know, I know! But what can I do?"

"Why not call in your advisers? We haven't met since the death of Ahaz. You'll remember, we were discussing making Lachish Jerusalem's outer defense, and constructing a water tunnel."

"All right. Then call a council meeting for tomorrow."

Differing in background and position, the counselors took their place—the general of the army, the chief treasurer, the high priest, Isaiah the prophet, the chief recorder, and several notable elders. The king had the power to do as he pleased, regardless of their recommendations, but Hezekiah willingly listened to their advice.

The men had thought about the matters discussed at their previous meeting and now brought their recommendations. "Lachish is on the main highway coming from the seacoast," the general stated. "It guards the only road that can accommodate large armies. If we fortify Lachish, we can block any army for weeks, perhaps permanently."

"That's right," Joah added. "I think we should strengthen Lachish."

The rest of the counselors agreed.

"Now let's discuss Jerusalem's water system," Hezekiah suggested, moving on to the next subject. "My engineers are ready to present their final plans."

The royal engineers unrolled their plans as the advisers gathered around the table. "The workmen will tunnel through from both sides at the same time," the chief draftsman explained. "This will cut construction time in half. We also plan to dig a reservoir right here"—he indicated the south side of the city—"to be named the Pool of Siloam ("sent")."

"That's an appropriate name," Shebna commented.

"Yes," the engineer said, "we thought it most fitting." Pointing again to the drawing, he continued, "The water will flow from the Gihon spring through the 1,200 cubit tunnel and into the Pool of Siloam."

"But how can we keep the Assyrians from entering the city through the tunnel?" Joah questioned.

"We will seal the Gihon end so no one from outside the city will have access to it. In fact, we will disguise it so no one will know there was once a spring there."

The counselors endorsed the plans, and not wasting any time, Hezekiah ordered the work to begin at once. Then the king broached another subject. "You all recognize our desperate need for freedom from the Assyrian yoke." Heads nodded here and there. "I believe you also know that several ambassadors are in Jerusalem requesting that we join in a united rebellion against Assyria. I believe the time is right to make such a move." The king paused, studying their faces. "How do you feel?"

"We ought to join," Shebna said.

"And this is a good opportunity," Joah commented, "what with Egypt in the alliance."

"Is Yahweh so weak that we must join the pagans?" Isaiah objected. The prophet's eyes blazed. "I could never agree to such a plan! Nothing will come but trouble and heartache. If we join this union, Assyria will carry us into exile. It would be national suicide!"

The general impatiently interrupted. "Isaiah, you're always warning of the dangers in alliances. But look, unless we get help from somewhere, we will die financially from paying exorbitant tribute every year."

"Why should we listen to that old man?" Shebna com-

plained. "Isaiah doesn't know anything about politics any-
way." He had always disliked the way Hezekiah favored the
prophet. It seemed to him that the king would do nothing
before he asked Isaiah for advice. The steward fancied himself the king's personal counselor, not Isaiah. The prophet, he
thought, was really usurping his authority.

Shebna had other reasons for taking a position against the
prophet. Although the highest official in the kingdom, he still
felt keenly his lack of noble birth. Since he had no family
tomb to show his importance, he was building one on the
Mount of Olives. And a fine tomb it would be, though expensive. The nation might be going bankrupt, but he insisted
on his ostentatious tomb so everyone would remember him.
Also Shebna enjoyed riding through the streets in his splen-
did chariot, never mind that it outshone the king's.

Isaiah had spoken to Shebna on behalf of Yahweh, rebuk-
ing the official's arrogance and predicting that the steward
would fall from power. The prophet had also revealed that he
and his extravagant chariot would go into a foreign land.
Shebna would die there, and his tomb would remain empty.

Yes, Shebna despised Isaiah and attacked the prophet at
every opportunity.

Hezekiah glared at the general and Shebna. "That 'old
man' of whom you speak is the prophet of Yahweh. We all
have a duty to heed the counsel of His messenger." Then, as
he adjourned the meeting for the day, he said, "Why not
think about it? Should we ally with these other nations or
not? Perhaps after a good night of sleep we can make a better decision."

"That's a good idea." Joah liked the idea of a delay, hoping the king would forget Isaiah's warning.

The counselors discussed the issue amongst themselves as
they departed. Couriers heading for Lachish hurried toward
the palace gate. The ambassadors from Ashdod halted in their

stroll in the royal garden to glance toward the Judah's elders, hoping for word on the outcome of the meeting. But no one noticed them.

Wanting to see where the Pool of Siloam would be, Joah threaded his way through the crowds toward the chosen spot on the southern side of the city. He noticed that the laborers had already begun to excavate.

The men worked in unison, their leader calling each stroke as their pickaxes struck the ground. The flat, hoe-like tools loosened the soil and broke the rocks into smaller pieces. Boys, girls, and women carried the debris in baskets balanced on their heads. The king's decree was only two hours old, and already the hole was half a cubit deep.

The work will not always go so fast, Joah mused. *When the men dig down to over their heads, they will have to hold the sides of the pool in place by woven mats.* He studied the area around the pit, visualizing the engineer's plans. When the men reached solid rock they wouldn't need any matting. Then the work would advance even more slowly.

Joah still could not forget the meeting. Why did Isaiah resist the other advisers? The recorder scratched his beard and rubbed the back of his neck. The prophet was so friendly, so humble and well mannered most of the time. And yet he often opposed the rest of the king's counselors. Whereas the other men reflected public opinion, Isaiah always went his own way. He refused to waver from what he called "the will of Yahweh." Could it be that fighting Isaiah was actually re-sisting . . . God? The court official hoped not. And yet, well, he'd have to think about it.

The streets seemed busier as Joah returned home. Everyone hoped to finish their chores before sunset. Then something brought him to an abrupt halt. In the marketplace a man strutted about, nearly naked, shouting to everyone passing by.

Siege at the Gates

"What is this?" Joah asked aloud. "Is this a lunatic? Maybe I should call one of the royal guards."

But it was no madman. As he approached he saw Isaiah preaching to anyone who stopped to listen. Why had he removed his clothes? But Joah didn't have long to wonder, for the prophet constantly explained himself to the crowd. He wailed like a doomed man. "Thus says Yahweh: If Judah allies with the heathen nations against Assyria, every one who hears my voice will be stripped as I am. You will be taken, naked, to Assyria with the other people who revolt against the great king."

Suddenly Joah understood Isaiah's earlier attitude. God, he mused, had revealed the calamity that would overcome Judah if she joined the other nations. Yahweh had already told the prophet that the allies would fail to win their freedom.

"That settles it!" Joah suddenly exclaimed out loud. His outburst attracted stares from several people nearby. Embarrassed, he headed toward home again. But he knew that he would side with Isaiah at the council meeting the next day.

On the following morning, though, several counselors still remained obstinate. Others, like Joah, had heard Isaiah's sermon in the marketplace and believed that the prophet was right. The king had not heard the sermon, but he too decided that Isaiah's counsel was correct. He would send the ambassadors home empty-handed.

The seasons passed. The confederacy revolted, and yet no word came of the invasion by Sargon. Travelers passing through Jerusalem daily brought news of the empire. The great king seemed to be busy elsewhere. He had no time to bother with the little kingdoms of Palestine.

Two years went by. The various political elements in Jerusalem who still favored the alliance grew stronger. They insisted that the continued peace proved Assyria too weak to put down the revolt. Perhaps the rebellion would actually succeed.

But Hezekiah refused to join. Although he wanted freedom as much as anyone, he still valued Isaiah's counsel. And the defenses of Jerusalem were not completed either. The granaries were full, the armories bulged, and a wall around part of the city had been strengthened. But the Siloam water tunnel was yet incomplete. Workmen had labored for two years, but the two crews still had not reached each other. Even when they did, much work would still remain before water could flow properly through the entire system.

But the unrest increased. Everyone longed for relief from the heavy taxes. They felt that anything would be better than Assyrian domination. As Judah's economic lifeblood seeped away, the nation slid toward bankruptcy.

But Hezekiah remained determined. "One day the people will know that I have chosen the best way," he confided to Shebna. "Then they will rejoice that Judah refused to join the pagans. The nations around us will be destroyed, one by one. Their people will die of starvation and disease during the long sieges; their cities will be laid waste, their women raped, their strong men slain, and their people deported to some distant land. Then Judah will see the wisdom of following the counsel of Yahweh, as Isaiah has given it. I pray constantly that I will not weaken and fall into the trap of running ahead of God."

"You may be right," Shebna muttered, "but I'll have to see it before I will agree with that old meddler." The steward departed, still refusing to accept Isaiah's position. He despised the prophet's power over the king, and his face flushed with anger at having lost another argument to Isaiah.

As Shebna neared the door, a messenger scurried into the chamber. Out of breath, and in great haste, he failed to bow to the king. "Sargon's armies are marching toward Palestine," the man gasped. "No one knows what nation he seeks to destroy."

The king glanced at Shebna, who had turned a ghastly white, and then asked about the size of the Assyrian forces.

"Without number, sir," the messenger answered. "Some estimate at least 100,000."

"Are there any military movements in the confederate nations?"

"Yes. The Egyptians move south to war against Nubia."

"I might have guessed," Hezekiah said, irritated. "I'm sure war with Nubia is more savory than war with Assyria. What about the Edomites and the Moabites?"

"They would rather pay taxes than fight."

"That leaves only the Philistine cities."

"That's right, my king. Ashdod will stand its ground. They think their city is unconquerable. And the other Philistine cities have pledged their support."

"I'm glad that we're not mixed up in this," the king sighed. "The Philistines are in for a massacre this time."

Sargon's forces entered Palestine along the coastal road leading south from Tyre and Sidon. As the great king neared Judah, people's fears mounted. Many worried that despite their loyalty, Sargon would invade Judah in search of booty to pay his troops. And their concerns proved true. The Assyrian gave little heed to Judah's loyalty to him. He overran every hamlet, mistreating and deporting the people, stealing and destroying property and animals along the way.

Hezekiah sent envoys to Sargon protesting his attack on a loyal subject, but it did no good. Jerusalem bulged as people fled the coastal plain. Everyone whispered of their dread that the enemy would cross the mountains and attack Jerusalem. But Sargon's target was the Palestinian confederacy. Even though most of the nations had already surrendered, Philistia still fought on, and he must punish her.

News arrived hourly in Jerusalem, brought by thousands of refugees. Every home harbored displaced persons from the west. The Philistine armies disintegrated before the relentless sword of Assyria, though the cities resisted. The invaders soon overcame and destroyed Gath, Ashdod, Ashkelon, and numerous minor villages. Some of them the Assyrians left in desolation, while others they placed under the control of kings who promised loyalty.

Jerusalem went to full alert. The city had no lack of manpower to prepare for a siege, for the farmers and merchants from outlying villages now swelled the defending forces to nearly double their normal strength. But the increased population also meant more mouths to feed, so the government crammed already full granaries with even more food. The tunnel had not yet been completed, so women filled every cistern and spare container. Endless lines of workers carried swords, spears, bows, and arrows to the tops of the city's walls.

Hezekiah appeared at the palace gate daily to encourage the people. "Judah has been faithful to Yahweh. We have followed His counsel. So if the Assyrians do come to Jerusalem, Yahweh will deliver us."

But suddenly all the preparations ceased. Merodach-bal-adari had conquered Babylon. By declaring himself king of Babylon, he proclaimed the city an independent state and thus asserted that it was no longer subject to Assyria. The Chaldean chieftain became an instant hero in Jerusalem. Anyone who opposed the hated Assyrians would naturally gain great popularity.

Within days Sargon finished at Ashkelon and, wasting no time with any other of the rich city-states, headed for Babylon. "Jerusalem is safe!" Shebna proclaimed.

"Praise to Yahweh!" Hezekiah breathed. "He protects His faithful people."

Chapter 8

Hezekiah
Draws His Sword

Sargon's hasty exit from Judah greatly relieved pressure on the nation. Now the fugitives could return to their villages. Many of them cursed Sargon for invading their land, but some were willing to mark it off as an error. So at Isaiah's insistence, Hezekiah continued to send tribute to Assyria. To raise the necessary funds, he taxed his own people heavily.

"Many people feel that Sargon double-crossed us," Hezekiah told Shebna one day.

"Exactly," the steward replied. "We're sending a fortune in taxes to Assyria with no visible benefits."

"I'm not sure about that, Shebna. The Assyrians have reduced international wars. And they've organized a strong central government that protects international trade."

The official shrugged. "That's true, but what's that when you see how ruthless they treat anyone who dares cross them?"

"I know." The king gazed out at the flowering bushes in the garden.

"This has lasted for almost 30 years," Shebna persisted. "And it's becoming critical." He produced a report of the national treasury. "Look, our country is nearly bankrupt! And the people grow more restless every day. They have seen the Assyrian army destroying our villages and killing our people when they should have protected us. Many of our people urge us to revolt."

Hezekiah had observed the international scene for 25

years now. "You know how swiftly the Assyrians deal with rebellious nations." The king put his hand on the steward's shoulder. "Sargon has reigned for 15 years, and I know that if we stopped the tribute he would knock on the gates of Jerusalem within months. No, Shebna. We will not withhold the taxes yet. We must wait for a more favorable time—perhaps when Sargon dies. And the new king? Dare we hope for a weaker one? At least we could pray that he will be powerless to punish us."

Meanwhile Hezekiah continued to strengthen his defenses. The water tunnel—called the tunnel of Siloam by some and Hezekiah's tunnel by others—was nearly complete. Thousands of workers had toiled for years on the project. The laborers expected soon to meet each other somewhere under the city. Then the water from Gihon would flow 1,200 cubits under the city to the artificial Pool of Siloam, just west of the king's gardens. The royal engineers had also constructed another reservoir within the gardens to store the overflow. Additional city walls went up around the pool and the king's gardens to doubly ensure their safety.

The royal servants rotated the stores in the granaries so that the grain was always fresh. The oldest supplies went to meet the city's current food needs, while the new harvests from the fields replaced them. That assured a fresh supply of food that would last for years should anyone attack Jerusalem.

The king strengthened every walled city in Judah, garrisoning it with soldiers and well-stocked storehouses in case of invasion from Assyria. But Lachish received more attention than the others. The citadel would guard the highway that led from the coastal plain to Jerusalem. For centuries literally every army attacking Judah had used it.

Already Lachish was the strongest fortified city of Judah—more substantial than the capital itself. It contained the royal retreat Ahaz had used, and should the situation demand, the king and his family could perhaps flee to there.

Hezekiah marveled at the strength of its walls—13 cubits thick, constructed of boulders weighing many tons each. Scores of towers studded the top, protruding over the edge and allowing the defenders opportunity to rain death upon any attacking army. Standing beside the massive gates, he gazed at the size of their cedar timbers. No battering ram could ever splinter those beams.

But he wasted little time in decorating the royal retreat, for he seldom stayed there. "These rooms remind me of my father," he told the architect. "I could never be comfortable here. But we must still maintain it. I may need it someday."

Sargon died in battle in Babylonia, but few in the world shed tears over his fate. His frequent campaigns had not endeared him to his subjects. Instead, they hated him, even rejoiced at his death. Perhaps a weaker king would follow. And perhaps they could have relief from the crushing war machine they detested so much.

But disappointment awaited them. Sennacherib, Sargon's oldest son, rode quickly to Dur Sharrukin, hoping to gain the throne before any of his numerous brothers wrested it from him. For several years Sennacherib had governed the province of Amid, and already his harsh policies had repulsed the world. He believed that Assyria ruled by divine right. His sole purpose for becoming king seemed to be to destroy his enemies.

Few who knew the young man needed to guess at his policies. Many had witnessed his insane delight in torturing his enemies to death. Fiendishly cruel, he impaled his captives atop pointed poles or skinned them alive. Careful political observers also recognized his inventive genius. He had developed several new building techniques. But he had also created more devastating war machines.

Unfortunately, Sennacherib easily rallied the Assyrians

around his banner and soon firmly implanted himself upon his father's throne. But Dur Sharrukin seemed too dull for him. Within months he moved his capital to ancient Nineveh, on the banks of the Tigris River. The old palace needed cleaning after 15 years of vacancy, but he remodeled it better than ever. The city walls he strengthened until they surpassed 50 feet in height and eight miles in length. Nineveh covered almost 2,000 acres, while Jerusalem comprised only 86.

Sennacherib had his engineers build an aqueduct to bring water from the mountains 30 miles away. He enlarged his palace to include more than 70 rooms and lined the walls with sculptured slabs of stone portraying the various conquests of the Assyrian kings. In his inscriptions he portrayed himself as the greatest of Assyrian rulers. Around the city he constructed a flooded moat, making Nineveh almost impregnable to any outside invader. With more than 120,000 people living there, Sennacherib had ample reason to refer to Nineveh as "my lordly city."

Hezekiah knew nothing of the Assyrian ruler's actions and character. He had long planned to rebel against the empire's tyranny, and now he felt the time had come. "I hope Sennacherib is a weak king," he told his council. "I hope his reactions to our resistance is slow." And so they made their decision. Judah would cease paying tribute.

But Hezekiah did not stop there. "We're going to need help, so I'm sending envoys to Sidon, Moab, Edom, Philistia, Egypt, and some of the other nations. I plan to form an alliance that will assure our success." The counselors, with the exception of Isaiah, concurred with the plan.

Most of the neighboring nations sided with Hezekiah. They, too, hated the Assyrian yoke and happily joined Judah against the despotic taskmasters of the Tigris.

As the most powerful king between Nineveh and Egypt, Hezekiah headed the confederacy. If he could resist

Siege at the Gates

Sennacherib, so, hopefully, could his neighbors. But not all accepted his leadership. Some of the Philistine city-states refused to join. Sargon had trounced them less than five years before, and they wanted no part in another invasion.

"These Philistines insult us by refusing to join," Hezekiah stormed. "We need the full cooperation of everyone in Palestine. If they won't join us willingly, then we'll have to use force." It took only a few days to organize his armies, and soon Hezekiah marched into Philistia, advancing on Ekron, the most important of the stubborn cities. Ekron's king, Padi, and his troops struggled bravely, but they proved no match for Judah's superior forces. Quickly Hezekiah overwhelmed Ekron's army and imprisoned Padi in Jerusalem for safekeeping. Then he installed several leading citizens as the town leaders. They willingly accepted Hezekiah's confederacy.

Judah's armies returned victoriously to Judah, Hezekiah riding in his royal chariot drawn by four black Egyptian mares. The tramp of thousands of marching feet and the rhythmic clank of swords and shields disappeared among the cheers of the vast crowds, impeding their progress. Their king had revolted against the hated Assyrians, refusing to pay the annual tribute. Now he had beaten their traditional enemies into submission. All along the route people chanted their favorite slogan for their favorite king: "Long live the king! Long live the king!"

The people of Judah had always loved Hezekiah. Now he had proved to be a noble warrior, and they thundered his praise. After the long march, the troops finally entered Jerusalem. The city had organized a great feast of victory.

The celebrations lasted far into the night, and the king was exhausted when at last he reached his private quarters. But he would not rest well that night. One awaited him who had no praise to give. Isaiah was not pleased with Hezekiah's new policies. He had always advised against confederacies with surrounding nations. While he was not disloyal to

Judah, he knew the agony that would come if the Assyrians invaded the land.

And Isaiah was not excited about the conquest of Ekron. "I understand your strategy, Hezekiah. You need the support of your people. And you need money to finance the military defenses. This victory won our nation's confidence, and the plunder has renewed your depleted treasuries. That you have done."

"If you could have seen how our soldiers fought, Isaiah," the king interrupted. "They mauled those Philistines!"

The prophet sadly looked at the exuberant, yet exhausted, king sitting on the stool beside his bed. "My dear friend," he warned, "Assyria is no Philistia. Sennacherib's armies can never be pushed around like Padi's platoons. Judah, for all her defenses and her valiant armies, is no match for the seasoned troops of Nineveh."

"But Isaiah . . ." Lapsing into silence, the king realized his arguments were futile.

"I have warned you, Hezekiah, of the risk of leaning on the promises of pagan nations." The prophet placed his hand on Hezekiah's shoulder. "Weak, unreliable, they would sooner surrender, join Sennacherib, and gobble Judah up than to fight the whip of Assyria."

"No, Isaiah"—the king held his hand up in protest—"these nations have promised me that they will join with me in this fight. I believe they will."

Still trying to reason with him, the graying prophet described how the Assyrians would destroy the land. "It's not too late, Hezekiah," he pleaded. "Why don't you send envoys to Sennacherib now? Why don't you reunite with the Assyrians before trouble overwhelms us?"

"No, my friend," the king answered kindly but firmly. "I have longed for freedom from Assyria for years. Now I have drawn my sword. I have chosen to revolt, and I will not turn back. May Yahweh protect His people."

Chapter 9

Snap of the Lion's Jaws

Isaiah's warnings still rang in Hezekiah's ears when word came that Sennacherib marched west along the King's Highway. *Does he plan war with Judah?* the monarch wondered. He had been "independent" for nearly four years now. For all his ruthlessness, the Assyrian king had been slow in punishing the rebellion.

No one knew for sure that Sennacherib intended to attack Judah, but Hezekiah sensed it. No doubt Nineveh's ruler had learned of Hezekiah's leadership role in Palestine.

"Don't worry," Shebna consoled as the king fretted over Sennacherib's approach. "Egypt has promised aid. All the Philistine cities have now pledged allegiance to you. Besides that, you have Moab, Edom, Tyre, and Sidon in your ranks."

"That's right," Hezekiah said, trying to encourage himself. "I need only to unite their armies with mine."

"Of course. Under Judah's brilliant generals, these armies will chase Sennacherib home like a dog with his tail between his legs."

Hezekiah smiled at the thought of the proud Assyrian army in full rout. The Judahite king had ruled for 28 years now. He had fostered the worship of Yahweh and encouraged the study of the writings of Moses and the prophets. Continually he had suppressed idolatry, destroying pagan altars and cult objects wherever he found them. And now he led a strong military alliance against the bloodthirsty tyranny of Assyria.

But one disturbing thought plagued his mind: Isaiah still insisted that dependence upon pagan nations would result in disaster. Trying to sort out his thoughts, the king strolled in the garden. The prophet always pleaded for dependence upon Yahweh. And Hezekiah believed that. But he thought Isaiah wrong this time. Every evidence indicated that he had been right in creating the confederacy.

Soon news flashed to Jerusalem by courier: "Sennacherib encamps before Sidon and demands total surrender."

"But Sidon belongs to our alliance," the king said in surprise. Then immediately regaining his composure, he realized he must act fast. "Now is the time for action," he ordered, turning to Shebna. "I understand that the terrain around Sidon is good for fighting, and with our superior numbers, the Assyrians won't stand a chance!"

The palace pulsated with life as dozens of messengers sped toward the various capitals of the Palestinian confederacy. The post bound for Sidon carried word of soon-coming help.

But Hezekiah's plan quickly collapsed. Instead of large armies, the "loyal" confederates dispatched only their regrets. Not one of the allies would commit troops to Sidon. "After all," they argued, "with Assyrians in the area we need our armies at home to protect our own people. Why should we go to fight for total strangers and risk the security of our own wives and children? Hezekiah is crazy if he expects such a thing." Obviously they had only joined hoping that Sennacherib would be afraid to launch an attack against them. But now that the enemy neared, they were in no mood to confront him in battle.

The worst blow was yet to come. Hezekiah's own army refused to fight on foreign soil. He pleaded with them, but to no avail. It became painfully evident that Sidon could expect no help from any source. The city was doomed.

The king of Judah sent his courier to apologize to Luli,

77

king of Sidon, but Luli would never receive the message. From a distant hill the messenger saw that the city had already fallen. People plodded in long lines, like oxen, toward Assyria and exile. Many poles stood around the city, bearing the corpses of impaled city officials. Dead bodies littered the fields and draped the tops of the city walls. He could do nothing but return with the terrible news.

Sennacherib cursed the gods of Sidon, for King Luli had escaped. The Assyrian scouts returned empty-handed. Nothing remained but to crown another in Luli's place. Ethba'al agreed to rule faithfully over those who remained in Sidon as well as the people from other lands who would re-settle there.

Then Sennacherib moved on to Tyre, but he soon wea-ried of capturing the island fortress. He had no ships and no equipment with which to construct a causeway—much to the joy of the city's defenders.

But before the Assyrians left the area, Sennacherib received envoys from Edom, Moab, and a number of the Philistine cities. The provinces had no desire to grapple with such a formidable foe. They had seen what he did to Sidon, and they wanted none of that. Deserting Hezekiah, they hurried to Sennacherib with their tribute, and he promised them peace.

The relentless Assyrian war machine moved south along the Mediterranean coastal plain to Ashkelon. Again, none of the allies would help. The city's defenders struggled valiantly, but in vain. In a few weeks the invaders broke through the walls, and Philistines perished by the hundreds. The soldiers slaughtered helpless women and innocent children as the Assyrians vented their fury on anyone who happened to be in their way.

At nightfall Ashkelon rested in Sennacherib's grip. Having captured King Sidqia alive, he tortured and sent him to Nineveh in chains. Rukibtu, a traitorous Philistine who had aided the Assyrians, received the throne. Hundreds of people in chains departed to exile in other parts of the empire. Corpses and desolation filled the streets of Ashkelon.

As Sennacherib finished Ashkelon, word arrived that King Shabaka of Egypt now approached. Shabaka, a Nubian, had answered Hezekiah's appeal—the only one willing to risk his army in the defense of another nation. Judah cheered Shabaka's arrival. Perhaps now the Assyrian would flee for home.

The two armies clashed at Eltekeh, near Ashkelon, and brave men struggled fiercely throughout the hot, dusty day. Blood flowed on both sides as the armies seesawed on the field. By evening, though, the Egyptian lines bulged, and soon all order collapsed as Judah's final hope retreated. At last night covered Eltekeh, and the sun sadly shut its eyes to the thousands of dead and dying from both sides. When the light of day again returned, the Egyptian army had vanished, leaving their dead and wounded to the mercy of the Assyrians.

But Sennacherib, quickly arranging for his own wounded, departed, abandoning Eltekeh with the dead and the Egyptian wounded still lying in the blazing sun. Buzzards and wild dogs quickly began their work as the army moved on to Ekron.

Governed by a council of local citizens, Ekron was no match for Assyria. Unorganized, weak from Hezekiah's recent siege, the city fell in a matter of days. The Assyrian ruler impaled the leaders while sparing the inhabitants. He knew they had been forced to join the Judahite rebellion against their will. The lord of Assyria promised to return King Padi to them on the condition that they would be loyal to Assyria. Then he turned to his real object—Judah.

Sennacherib had employed a tactic used by every Assyrian king in history. He first weakened a major power by destroying its allies, eliminating every source of help so that his target would lie vulnerable to his armies.

The great king knew that nothing would hinder him in dissecting Judah at his leisure. He had put Sidon, Philistia, and Egypt out of the fight. Moab, Edom, and others had withdrawn. Now Hezekiah stood alone.

The majority of the Judean villages lay defenseless. The country contained only 47 walled cities and towns to protect the people living in the countryside. But even the walled towns could not withstand experts in siege warfare.

Sennacherib divided his army into small raiding parties that he sent throughout Judah to mop up every town and village. "Show no mercy," he instructed his general. "Slay anyone who resists you. Capture everyone who will surrender, whether they be men, women, or children, old or young. Seize all their animals and every treasure you can carry. Send it all to Assyria. We must assure that Judah will never trouble my empire again. I will transplant its people to a dozen different countries. The nation will disappear from the earth."

Hezekiah's armies met the Assyrians in battle but retreated in complete defeat. The king and a small band of survivors managed to reach Jerusalem. But Judah had lost most of its fighting men and all of its horses and chariots.

In less than a month the Assyrians regrouped. They had captured 45 walled towns and every open village and had rounded up more than 200,000 people, sending them half naked and chained together in long mournful columns to Assyria. Also they had transported livestock without number to Nineveh, together with every other valuable they could loot.

Only two cities yet awaited capture: Lachish and Jerusalem. "Jerusalem is the capital," Sennacherib decided. "I will leave it until last. We will besiege Lachish first, and then no power on earth can save Jerusalem."

While Sennacherib carved up Judah's allies, Hezekiah suffered constantly. Not only did he grieve at the terrible events but he had developed an excruciating boil. The physicians tried to relieve his pain, but he refused to rest. "How can I lie here while my country is overrun by an enemy?" he protested. "I must work out some plan to save my people."

But physical pain was the least of Hezekiah's troubles. Mental anguish over the fate of Judah threatened to overwhelm him. Daily he lay on his face in the Temple, weeping, praying, fasting for hours. He scolded the royal guards stationed in Jerusalem, but they refused to leave the capital again to save anyone else.

"The soldiers are convinced that the Assyrians have superior weapons," he told Shebna. "Their battle chariots each contain a driver, two spearmen, and an archer. We have lost our chariots. Now we simply have nothing to stop them."

"And the Assyrians have cavalry, too," Shebna reminded him. "We can no longer boast of a single horse for an officer to ride. All the horses we have left are reserved for the messenger service."

"And that's not all the soldiers say," the king continued. "The enemy has iron weapons, while ours are bronze. 'It would be suicide,' they say, 'to leave Jerusalem. These walls are our only advantage.'" Discouragement tinged his voice. "They should know better than that. We have known the Assyrians to destroy walls quite similar to ours. But still the soldiers place their trust in stone. The Assyrians can kill and capture our people by the hundreds of thousands, but they will stand idly by and wait. 'When the enemy comes here,' they say, 'then we will fight.' It's ridiculous—no, it's criminal!"

Hezekiah knew that when Sennacherib reached Jerusalem it would be too late for his armies to save them. Only Yahweh could deliver them then.

As he had waited for the Assyrians to reach Jerusalem, Hezekiah had studied every movement of the enemy. *There is no doubt that his objective is Jerusalem,* he had reasoned to himself. *Except for some miracle, Sennacherib will soon lay siege to the holy city.*

Messengers arrived from the battlefront daily, describing the relentless advance. They had reported the fall of Sidon, and the tyranny of Moab, Edom, and several other Philistine cities. Hezekiah had fumed over the lack of unity among his allies and bemoaned his inability to organize an effective resistance.

Through it all, another problem wedged its way into Hezekiah's mind: What would happen to his family? Surely Sennacherib would most likely attack Jerusalem first, just as he had Sidon and Ashkelon. Once he conquered the capital, he would probably return home. But what would become of his wives, concubines, and daughters if they fell into Assyrian hands? Cold chills swept over him as he thought of them in the clutches of such an evil enemy. They would receive horrible treatment from such a heartless foe. Probably they would be raped, maybe even butchered before his eyes. That was often the policy of conquering kings, especially the Assyrians who used terror itself as one of their most effective weapons. Hezekiah couldn't bear the thought. He had to do something to assure their safety.

So while Sennacherib occupied himself with the extensive siege at Ashkelon, he decided that the royal retreat held the answer to his family's needs. "Lachish is far stronger than Jerusalem," he explained to them. "Even Sennacherib couldn't break into that fortress."

As a result he decided to send his entire family to Lachish—except for 7-year-old Prince Manasseh and Hephzibah, the child's mother. "You will be safe there," he assured them. "If Sennacherib captures Jerusalem, he could do no greater harm to the royal family than to slay me, Hephzibah, and our son. But you, my wives and daughters, will be safe. Most likely they'll completely forget about you."

The plan had taken form over several days. One evening,

under cover of darkness, Hezekiah gathered his family together for the last time. He explained once again why they must not remain in Jerusalem. But in spite of the king's assurances, the women and children had become fearful. They had heard of what Assyria did to its victims. But they must go, for Hezekiah had spoken. The night was young as they left Jerusalem under the care of four regiments of the king's handpicked soldiers. The men were under oath to remain in Lachish and guard the king's family with their lives. Hezekiah didn't realize, on that sad night of parting, that he would never see his wives and daughters again.

Once his family safely reached Lachish, Hezekiah puzzled over Sennacherib's movements. "Why doesn't he advance on Jerusalem?" he demanded in frustration. "I'm his target. I'm the key to this confederacy." But the king soon recognized the enemy's strategy: Sennacherib intended to destroy all help before attacking Judah itself.

Daily Hezekiah prayed in the Temple. And daily he received news of the progress of the enemy troops. The rejoicing over the arrival of help from Egypt turned to mourning at word of its defeat. As Egypt's forces dissolved like clouds before a hot desert wind, Hezekiah remembered Isaiah's epitaph—"Egypt is a broken reed." Judah's last earthly hope was gone. Only Yahweh could save them now.

Ekron collapsed, and soon the Judean countryside crawled with Assyrian soldiers, plundering, destroying, killing, taking captive. Half-naked Judahites, chained by the thousands—men, women, children, old and young—choked the roads, trudging the long thirsty miles to the land of the Tigris River. Hundreds would never survive the journey.

Many captives passed within sight of Jerusalem, where they could see their beloved Temple. "Why has Yahweh forsaken us?" they wailed. "Why the shame?"

The sight of his people herded into captivity tore at

83

Siege at the Gates

Hezekiah's heart, but he couldn't persuade his troops to rescue them. They were willing to man the ramparts and carry news. But leave Jerusalem to fight? Never! Selfishly they watched while hundreds of thousands of their people passed into exile.

Hezekiah could hardly believe what was happening. "Sennacherib carves up Judah at his leisure," he complained to Eliakim, Shebna's secretary. "And yet Jerusalem—except for its swollen population—continues as though nothing is happening. My pleas fall on deaf ears. They will defend their own city if they have to. But please don't ask them to leave their walls. Are they not their brothers' keepers?"

And alas, too late, Hezekiah realized the enemy's scheme. "The Assyrians do not march directly on Jerusalem," he despaired. "They will take Lachish first after destroying every other city. Yahweh forbid!" His heart sank. "I've sent my family into the lion's jaws!"

The citizens of Lachish saw the inevitable even as Hezekiah did and prepared for the task the city had been built to do. It was the strongest fortification in Palestine and had the best troops to defend it. Lachish rested in a mountain pass, about 25 miles southwest of Jerusalem. Every major army in history had passed that spot before approaching the holy city, and Sennacherib was no exception. The Assyrians feared to leave such a well-manned fortress behind them. The city must be eliminated.

In traditional Assyrian style, altered somewhat by the military genius of Sennacherib, the siege began. The army surrounded the city, blocking every exit, every hope for help. Assyrian soldiers worked behind monster shields that arched over their heads, protecting them from the arrows and rocks hurled at them from the walls. Thousands of men toiled for days to pile rocks, mud, sticks, and other debris against the wall. Gradually they constructed a sizable ramp that would permit their troops to reach the top of the wall.

Eventually they would use scaling ladders to enter the city. But ladders were too dangerous now. The soldiers needed to weaken the city first, so Sennacherib ordered his battering rams to begin their work. Most armies would have used battering rams on the gates or on the walls at ground level. But on a fortified city like Lachish, weeks and months of battering would have caused little damage. As a result the Assyrians mounted their battering rams on wheels so they could push them up the ramp. That way the rams pounded on the upper portion of the wall, which soon began to crumble.

Manning the rams was dangerous work, for the city's defenders bombarded them with arrows, rocks, flaming brands— anything to stop their work. To draw attention away from the rams, the Assyrians unleashed a constant cloud of arrows into the city. They intended to kill or wound as many of the defenders as they could, for Lachish could never replace them. The invaders used slingers, who hurled fist-sized stones over the wall by the thousands at speeds that could severely wound anyone struck by them. Larger slings tossed rocks over the walls to batter down houses and kill the people.

Sennacherib employed his most devious method to break a strong wall. Men tunneled under it, shoring it with huge timbers to keep the excavation from collapsing and to hold up the wall. When they had dug under one section of the wall, they set fire to the timbers. As the wood burned, it weakened and collapsed. With all support suddenly gone, the wall crumbled, allowing the enemy to enter.

All this took time, but Sennacherib was patient. "I will stay here until I have reduced the city to rubble," he boasted. "These people will be duly chastised."

"How long will it be before Lachish falls?" a servant asked

"I don't know." His eyes narrowed to slits, and his jaw stiffened. "But of one thing I am certain . . . it will fall!"

Chapter 10

Desperate
Ride for Peace

Jerusalem's mood was hard to understand. In spite of the nearly 200,000 Judahites that had been deported, with every hamlet, town, and field destroyed, the city continued with business as usual. Merchants bought and sold as though no war existed. The only sign of danger was the presence of troops on the walls and the continual scurrying of couriers.

But news of the siege of Lachish began to make its impact. Now few people appeared on the streets, caravans disappeared, foreigners departed, and merchants stayed put. Time had run out, it seemed. Jerusalem would be next. The Assyrians would come, level its walls, and slaughter or exile every citizen.

Sick with fever from his boil, discouraged by the constant setbacks, Hezekiah found his mind racing in an endless, vicious circle. *Lachish lies under siege. Lachish . . . my wives and daughters are there. Lachish . . . I thought it was impregnable. Lachish . . . it's all but gone now . . . the Assyrians are about to capture it . . . to kill my loved ones or take them away. What more could they do but take my life?*

Beaten down by grief, worry, and loneliness, Hezekiah decided to go again to pray in the Temple. "Yahweh has protected me all my life," he told his servants. "Why has this calamity come now? I must know."

But the king could hardly stand because of his physical suffering. Several servants carried him to the Temple. Placing him in the shade of an overhanging balcony, they stepped aside to allow him privacy. Others also prayed nearby. Some recognized him and wondered at his weakened condition. Thinking of his need for Yahweh's deliverance, the king paid them no attention. A burden of guilt overwhelmed him. "Could I be at fault?" he prayed. "Are the people paying for my transgression?"

Against the specific counsel of Isaiah, ignoring the prophet's warnings, he had led Judah into war with Assyria. "Was I wrong to refuse to follow Yahweh's servant?" Immediately he knew the answer. "All Judah suffers because of my sin," he moaned to himself.

Paying no attention to those watching, the king wept. Sweat beaded on his brow, then rolled down into his beard in rivulets. "What a fool I've been! And now even my family will pay for my sin." His heart yearned for forgiveness. "O Yahweh, please hear me . . . please forgive me. Please heal my body, mind, and soul . . . please bring us relief from Assyria!"

Suddenly Isaiah pushed through the crowd. Hezekiah had been praying and weeping for hours, but not even his nearest servant had understood what he said. But now the prophet approached to answer him. The restlessness of those around him drew the king's gaze from the ground on which he lay. When the prophet bowed in respect, Hezekiah motioned for him to rise. "What is the word from Yahweh?"

For a moment Isaiah hesitated, then when he spoke, only the king heard his voice. "You have been correct, Hezekiah. Yahweh has allowed the Assyrians free access to Judah."

"But why?"

"Because you trusted in the surrounding nations rather than in God. Yahweh warned you, but you did not listen. Now Judah is desolate, and Jerusalem lives in fear."

"But, friend," Hezekiah pleaded, "are we to die?"

Siege at the Gates

"No," the prophet assured him. "God has granted you pardon. You have served faithfully all your life. Only in your desire to ally with other nations have you sinned.

"Now Yahweh says, 'Send an envoy to Sennacherib, seeking terms of peace. Surrender to him at once. Accept whatever terms he asks. If you fail to do this, he will destroy Jerusalem.'"

The king cringed at paying more tribute, but it was his only hope. "I will do it at once," he assured Isaiah.

Hezekiah's aides carried him back to the palace. But he could not rest. Impatiently he sent for Shebna. "Go to Sennacherib at once," he commanded. "Ask for his terms of peace."

The steward paled at the king's order. "Peace?" he exclaimed. "Have you gone mad? Don't you know that Sennacherib impales the officials of a conquered nation?"

"Yes, I know of the cruelty of Sennacherib. But that's why you must ask the terms of peace. Take other officials with you and go. Present your message only to Sennacherib. Then return to Jerusalem with his answer. I will pray for your safe return."

"As the king wishes," Shebna conceded, his hands trembling as he left.

Only after the envoys departed for Lachish would Hezekiah take the sleep potion given him by his physicians. Soon the king dozed in a fitful slumber. He dreamed of his wives and children, waking occasionally from nightmares of Assyrian brutality and from the pain of the boil.

Shebna took Eliakim and one other man with him, leading his group past the construction site of his tomb for a last-minute inspection. In spite of the danger from marauding Assyrian soldiers, he had insisted that the crews stay on the job, allowing them a watchman farther up the hillside to warn of the approach of any danger.

The devastation they saw on their journey appalled the men. Every town had been burned out and destroyed. Bodies rotted everywhere, and the stench would have sickened the hardiest warrior. "I wonder what we'll find at Lachish," Eliakim wondered aloud to his colleagues. "Will the city still exist? Will we be permitted to speak to the king?"

"Even more important than that," Shebna interrupted, "will we ever come back alive?"

"I'm sure we will," Eliakim tried to encourage them. "But I wonder if the Assyrians will accept anything but total destruction?"

Night crept in from the east and forced them to bed down under an overhanging ledge. "Travel by night is too dangerous," Shebna complained, "even on an urgent mission like ours."

They slept in shifts, keeping watch lest a prowler, or animal, or the Assyrians take them unawares. Eliakim noticed that Shebna seemed more concerned for his chariot than for his companions. Sunrise found the envoys on their way again. Only a few more furlongs to Lachish. As they crossed the final hill they gasped at the panorama they viewed. Thousands of men worked to breach the city walls. "They have not yet broken through," Eliakim rejoiced, "but it looks like they will soon."

The harsh command of a guard just up the road interrupted them. Nervously he approached them, his sword drawn, interrogating them in the Syrian language. They showed him their official identification and asked to see the great king.

Still searching to see if the envoys might be armed, the guard relaxed the grip on his sword but did not return it to its scabbard. He hesitated, eyeing them closely, and then bowing politely, motioned them to follow him. Shebna's driver urged his steeds on. The Assyrian guard remained wary

89

but treated them with courtesy. He led them to his superior officer before returning to his post.

As cautious as the guard and much less friendly, the Assyrian officer at least showed no inclination to harm them. When they explained their mission, he directed them to park their chariot and rest, while he arranged for their audience. They were now behind a low hill so they could no longer observe the city. But they could hear the shouts, the twang of the giant slings, the thuds of the battering rams, and the occasional cry of the injured in the battle.

A few minutes later the officer returned and motioned for them to follow him. Leaving their chariot in the care of an Assyrian guard, they accompanied their guide. Shebna glanced back to make sure his chariot was safe. The envoys judged that they had walked nearly halfway around the city by the time they topped a hill overlooking Lachish. Sennacherib's portable throne dominated the summit. It resembled a miniature castle on wheels. Carved with cult symbols and depictions of previous battles, the throne had a fringed canopy shielding it. Overlaid with gold, the throne appeared to be extremely heavy—proved by the team of eight black stallions tended by a slave under a nearby shelter. Servants scurried everywhere, bringing this or that to the king at his bidding. Some fanned him, others prepared or presented water, wine, or food, according to his desires.

Sennacherib watched the progress of the siege and sent messages to his generals. At the same time he received news from, and dispatched orders to, different parts of his empire. The place was a whirlwind of activity.

The officer's instructions to step in front of the king rudely reminded them of their mission. "Bow with your faces in the dust," he whispered. "The king will speak to you when he is ready. Then, and not until then, you should rise and speak to him."

Shebna and his companions slipped into position and bowed. They cringed at paying homage to a pagan king, but the safety of Jerusalem and Lachish depended on them.

It seemed that hours passed before the king granted them permission to rise. Staggering to their feet, they flexed their cramped muscles. Startled at the anger in his eyes, they prayed that Yahweh would grant them mercy.

"What do you want from me?" The Assyrian ruler half spat, half laughed, the words.

Trembling, Shebna presented Hezekiah's message. "The king of Judah is sorry that he has caused trouble to the king of Assyria," he began. "He desires peace with my lord. Will the great king end his siege of Lachish and tell King Hezekiah his terms of peace? Whatever you request, Judah will be most pleased to do."

The Assyrian exploded into laughter—so fierce, so evil, that Shebna's flesh crawled. He wondered how anyone could expect mercy from a man such as this. But he refused to give up hope.

The Assyrian's laughter finally calmed enough for him to speak. "Why has Hezekiah suddenly become so repentant? Is it not because Judah lies in ruins? Of course! He has come to the end of his hope." Again the king laughed. "Hezekiah knows that I will crush him, so he begs for mercy."

Sennacherib's humor iced into sneering hatred. "Hezekiah deserves no mercy!" he thundered. "Nevertheless"—the laughing continued at intervals—"I, the great king of Assyria, will show that wretched Jew that I extend mercy to the most undeserving. We will stop the war when Hezekiah meets my terms—and not until."

Perhaps, Shebna reasoned, his hope reviving, there was yet a chance to save Jerusalem and Lachish. But his hopes plummeted when Sennacherib decreed, "To stop the war Hezekiah must pay 30 talents of gold and 300 talents of silver."

Siege at the Gates

It was nearly an impossible sum for Judah, but that was not all. Sennacherib insisted he would not end the siege of Lachish until he had received the money in full. "When I have the money I will go home. Then Hezekiah can have what is left of his kingdom. Lachish could fall any day," the Assyrian ruler jeered. "Hurry now, if you expect to save it."

The envoys retraced their steps to their chariot and Shebna found to his delight that nobody had touched it. Clambering aboard, they dashed toward Jerusalem, the king's laughter still ringing in their ears. Nightfall did not stop them now, even though danger lurked at every turn. As the horses stumbled on in the darkness the men silently hung on, each lost in his own thoughts.

Dawn was breaking when they caught sight of Jerusalem, still wrapped in slumber. Shebna bypassed his tomb now. The king must have his report immediately. The gatekeepers admitted them at once, knowing the importance of their mission.

The palace still slept, but a servant awakened the king. Shebna explained the terms of peace, and the monarch paled as he rose from his bed. "Where can we find that kind of money in time to save Lachish? O Lord God, help us. My family!"

Sinking back in despair, he realized that raising such a sum seemed impossible, but he would try. Instantly he ordered his financial advisers to tap every source. Shebna and his fellows started home to rest, but if the king had his way, they would have little sleep.

Joah hurried to weigh the gold and silver of the treasury, but the king's coffers didn't hold enough. Even when servants had brought all the gold and silver in the Temple treasury, it still was inadequate.

The king's servants approached the wealthy merchants and landowners, but they refused to donate. In final desperation, servants removed the gold from the doors and hinges of the Temple—a time-consuming process. It finally added enough to meet Sennacherib's demands.

When word reached his ears, Hezekiah sighed. "It has taken too long," he exclaimed. "Four days have passed, and the Assyrians have been beating away at Lachish. I'm afraid it's too late to save my family."

But Shebna and his aides arrived within minutes, and seconds later they dashed toward Lachish, leading a caravan of donkeys bearing the tribute. As they disappeared, Hezekiah returned to his bed and prayed for their safe journey. He prayed that the tribute would arrive in time to save Lachish . . . to save his family from doom.

Chapter 11

Fire Under the Wall

The din of battle filled the air as Sennacherib inspected the work of his armies. His chariot could not make the complete tour in such rough terrain, so he rode his favorite stallion. The ramp against the walls now approached to within six cubits of the top of the southwest corner wall, and the battering rams had broken it down so that his men could enter. But the large number of Judahite solders clustering near the breaches prevented that.

On the west side, flooded by the afternoon sun, Sennacherib watched in anticipation. At the base of the wall, protected from the prying eyes and deadly arrows of Lachish's defenders, workers had nearly completed undermining the wall. Great timbers supported the tunnel and the wall itself. When the tunnel was finished, the Assyrians would cover the timbers with pitch, pack them with brush, and set everything afire. As the beams disintegrated, they would leave the wall unsupported, causing it to crumble.

Riding on farther, the Assyrian monarch observed his archers sending never-ending volleys over the wall. Slingers and giant catapults supported them. The constant shower of arrows, stones, and rocks caused many casualties in the city, further weakening its defenses.

The siege had already lasted several weeks, and Sennacherib knew that the enemy would soon offer little resistance. "Now that I think of it," he commented, turning to a general, "the men on the wall seem sluggish. Perhaps it is time to push into the city."

"How about tomorrow?" the officer asked.

"Yes! Tomorrow will be the day. We must finish Lachish before Hezekiah's men return. Why should we leave without capturing the city?"

"That's right," the Rabshakeh, his cupbearer and a high official in his administration, added. "We wouldn't want to miss all the treasure and slaves in Lachish." They laughed as they thought of Hezekiah's expression as he heard the news that they had taken his strongest city.

"So . . . ready or not, people of Lachish," Sennacherib triumphantly announced, "tomorrow we enter your city!"

Few men slept that night. The boredom of the siege had left every soldier in a constant state of frustration. Soon each man could vent his rage on those cursed defenders that had made life so difficult during the past few weeks. Many Assyrians had perished during the siege. Now would come revenge—and plunder.

Long before daylight a red glow flickered along the western wall. To the city's defenders it appeared to be a fire coming from below the wall, but they could not see its source. More Judahite troops moved to the top of the wall to defend it. Meanwhile they continued to carefully guard the breaches in the other walls.

The long siege had worn the people's nerves to a raw edge. Every man must fight to defend the city. Even women who had no families had taken their places on the wall. But their frustration increased as they realized they could do little against the attackers. The Assyrians were well protected, and only the careless enemy soldier got wounded or killed. And yet the continuous stream of missiles hurtling over the walls randomly killed or injured their people. No one could safely venture into the streets.

The black smoke spread its omen over the western wall, and courage evaporated. "How can we last much longer?"

more and more exclaimed. "Half our people are wounded or dead, and others are sick from exhaustion, starvation, and disease. Will this war never end? Will help never come?"

The members of the royal family were especially fearful.

"I hear that families of kings are tortured and slain," one of Hezekiah's wives whispered to the others. "Can we expect any mercy from these barbarians?"

"I doubt it," another answered. "And I've also heard how Assyrians systematically rape every woman in a city."

The first looked aghast at her companion. "If they break through the walls, do you think . . ."

"I don't know. Perhaps we should gather everyone together and pray."

The women prayed for help and pleaded with their guards to protect them. They sent messages to Hezekiah that they knew would never get beyond the walls. Only the calm of the older women and the presence of the royal guards prevented complete hysteria.

The rising sun had begun to tint the sky with red and gold as the Assyrians moved into attack formation under the cover of the lingering darkness or behind nearby hills so that Lachish would see nothing until it was too late to counterattack. The smoke of the fire still curled skyward. The military engineers saw that the timbers would collapse within the hour, and they notified the king. Sennacherib, in his best humor for months, ordered the attack to begin as soon as the wall crumbled.

The largest force assembled near the expected site of collapse. Other well-trained units prepared to scale the wall at other breaches. Several commando units would scramble over the walls to open the city gates for the rest of the army. Plans had been laid . . . the army waited . . . the smoke boiled upward. Every soldier prepared to pounce on the helpless city.

Suddenly a cry came from atop the western wall as the

great 13-cubit-thick wall of man-sized boulders trembled and collapsed in a cloud of dust. Dozens of defending soldiers tumbled with it into a crumpled heap. Instantly the Assyrians leaped into action. Converging on the opening in the wall, they climbed over the breaks made by the battering rams and soon streamed through the gates opened by advance scouts.

Stunned by the destruction of its wall, the city had little fight left in it. A few held out for a time, but most were easy prey for the Assyrians—some instantly slaughtered, others herded as prisoners.

The shrieks of the wounded, the dying, and the pursued shattered the air. Children ran, women sought any hiding place. But no one escaped the invaders. The wails of helpless women filled the city.

Resistance ended quickly, as thousands of Assyrians continued to pour into the little city. Most of the soldiers turned from fighting to roam through the city, looting and raping. But the struggle at the royal retreat continued. Hezekiah's personal bodyguard refused to surrender. Because of sheer desperation, the guards and retainers fought better than the invaders. Five or six Assyrians perished for every one of the royal guards. Sennacherib had entered the city now, and he wondered why they still held out so fiercely when the city had already fallen. Could someone important live within the citadel walls?

His eyes rested upon the shield hanging between the arches of the portico. "The royal symbol of Judah!" he mused out loud. "Could Hezekiah be here?" For several minutes he stood in confusion. "No, he couldn't be here. He sent his envoys from Jerusalem. But someone of the royal household must certainly be here, or these men would never put up such a fight."

Turning to an officer standing nearby, Sennacherib ordered, "I don't care who lives here. I want them alive. They will make impressive trophies."

Siege at the Gates

More reinforcements arrived, and the palace guards perished one by one. But Assyrian corpses surrounded their bodies. The last guard died, and the soldiers surged toward the door, filled with greed, lust, and anger. Instantly a command stopped them. "Halt!" Sennacherib himself shouted the order, his voice ringing above the bedlam. The men knew they must heed it or die.

Quickly they turned to face their king. In their zeal to conquer the city's last stronghold they had failed to see him arrive. They felt like children caught in a misdeed. No matter that they had just won a glorious victory; in Sennacherib's presence they became only chattel for him to spend on his whims . . . to throw away for his honor.

"You have done well," the king said gruffly, "but this is a royal house, and you are not to harm anyone who lives here. These people should be gently led to Nineveh. I will arrange their fate myself when I reach my lordly city."

The sun by now had ridden its flaming chariot into the heavens, the final assault having taken only five hours. Sennacherib, occupying his portable throne overlooking the devastated city, surveyed the tribute and the captives marching before him. He had spared the lives of what he now knew to be Hezekiah's wives. "They will make excellent additions to my own harem," he decided, ordering the safe journey of his royal prizes. He would send his personal servant to assure their protection. The women would ride in carts, while the majority of the prisoners would walk the 400 miles.

Attendants surrounded the king's throne. Two servants fanned from behind to cool him and to brush away the flies. Scribes recorded all the wounded, killed, and captured. They also listed every article of value taken from the city, noting the cattle, goats, sheep, and oxen to be herded toward Nineveh.

The elders of Lachish sprawled before the king, their

faces in the dust. They had lain there for an hour before Sennacherib bothered to recognize them. "Have mercy upon the people of Lachish," their leader begged. "Please spare their lives and leave them here in their own land." The king's laughter drowned his pleas. It grated even Sennacherib's calloused attendants. "Of course I will have mercy. Haven't you heard? I am the most merciful king ever to come to Judah. You should thank me for delivering your people from Hezekiah. I have spared many of them already. If I hadn't stopped them, my soldiers would have slain everybody. Mercy? Of course!

"You needn't worry yourselves about the people," the king said, his voice suddenly smooth. "I'll take them to a better country than this. They'll be all right. The only people who will be executed now are your elders!" With vicious laughter he motioned to his soldiers to begin their work.

Many of the king's attendants, though often forced to view such carnage, turned from the gory sight. Some of the city leaders were beheaded, some impaled on long, stout poles thrust upright into holes in the ground, leaving the men suspended on top to die. Others the Assyrians skinned alive or tortured until they died of physical shock. Scribes dutifully recorded each execution for official documents.

While Sennacherib reveled in the executions, Shebna and his men topped a rise not far away. They had hoped to find Lachish still holding out. But they had already realized that all hope had vanished. Streams of men, women, and children chained together had met them on the road, with the Assyrians goading them along like animals. Several times Hezekiah's delegation barely escaped capture. But for their official papers they too would have been trudging toward Assyria.

Still they were unprepared for the sight of Lachish. Dense clouds of smoke veiled the burning buildings, with bodies sprawled everywhere, and still more captives staggered from a hill to their left, where they could see the Assyrian king's throne.

"We have no time to lose," Shebna shouted. "We must get to Sennacherib at once. Perhaps we can get him to release the captives."

"I hope so," Eliakim replied. "Hezekiah met his peace terms." But when they entered the Assyrian king's presence, horror and despair washed over them. Scattered before the monarch were the bloody remains of more than a dozen old men. The envoys could scarcely keep from vomiting. A guard ordered them to grovel before the king. Again they lay in the dust waiting for him to receive them.

At last Sennacherib conceded to acknowledge them. "What have you to say?" he thundered. "Will Hezekiah surrender and become my captive?"

"Surrender? Captive?" Shebna slowly echoed the terrible words. "Nothing was said about Hezekiah becoming a captive! We brought the tribute you demanded—30 talents of gold and 300 of silver."

The Assyrian ruler's laugh shivered down their spines. "Good! You have brought me gifts. But the tribute will not be enough. If Jerusalem is as wealthy as Lachish, perhaps I'll take her too. Of course," he grinned, "if Hezekiah surrenders, there will be less bloodshed!"

Then with a scowl he added, "I will take the money you have brought. But I must have Jerusalem too." Suddenly he shouted, "Go tell that Jew that Sennacherib the Great will come to Jerusalem! Tell him he must surrender the city, or I will destroy it!"

Chapter 12

The Sign in the Sundial

Hezekiah watched the envoys ride through the gate on their way to Lachish. His heart longing for relief from the invasion, he wondered about his family and hoped his message would be in time.

As he entered his bedchamber his constant pain again stabbed into his consciousness. For a couple of hours the speeding of the tribute to Sennacherib had occupied his thoughts. But now he once more felt the agony of the boil. The royal surgeons had lanced it several times, and yet it always returned.

The king's strength ebbed. "If he is ever to recover," insisted one of the doctors, "he must have some rest."

"It might help," another suggested, "if we give him something that will ease his pain and induce sleep."

At first Hezekiah had refused the medication. But now that the envoys had gone to Sennacherib, he had done everything within his power to achieve Jerusalem's safety. The exhausted king now permitted his doctors to administer their potions.

"The boil has worsened," the chief physician worried out loud. "The king has been too busy. He hasn't let us cleanse and redress the wound often enough."

"And now infection has set in," his associate added. "It affects his entire system."

"In fact," his chief agreed, "he has developed a fever. We must act quickly to save his life."

The sedatives took effect as the doctors worked to reduce the fever and release more pus. They concentrated so closely on their work they didn't see another man enter the room.

Isaiah knew that Hezekiah was desperately ill, having often come to bring warnings and counsels from Yahweh. But today he had no desire to deliver his message. While he had no fear for his own safety, yet he loathed to hurt his friend with what he now had to say.

Slipping to Hezekiah's side, Isaiah touched his hand. As the surgeons stepped back, the king opened his eyes, and his lips curved in a smile as he recognized his old friend.

"Isaiah . . . I'm so glad to see you." He assumed that the man of God had good news. Perhaps Sennacherib would spare his family, he hoped. Perhaps Yahweh would heal him. Perhaps . . . His thoughts stumbled over one another. But as Isaiah spoke he clung to each word.

"Hezekiah . . ." The prophet lingered over the name. "The Lord has revealed that you will not recover. You must use your strength to set your house in order. Make out your will so everything can be done as you want. Confess your sins and make sure of your salvation." The older man paused, his hand on his friend's brow. "You must also name the next king and instruct him in your plans. Hezekiah"—tears lurked in the prophet's voice—"set your house in order, for you will die and not live."

The ruler's shocked expression blended with the tears of a weeping prophet and the surprise of the doctors. No one said anything. After what seemed an eternity, Isaiah squeezed his friend's trembling hand and left. The physicians departed to discuss the change in events, leaving Hezekiah alone . . . alone with his thoughts . . . alone with his message of doom. "'Put your house in order, Hezekiah.'" The words stung his soul. "'You will die and not live, Hezekiah.'" It seemed like some horrible dream—no, nightmare! *But why? How can*

Yahweh forsake me at a time like this? Uncontrollable sobs wracked him. Turning his face to the wall, he wept like a child.

Lord, . . . why? He demanded. *Haven't I been faithful? Haven't I led Judah to worship You? I've even sanctified the Temple and destroyed all the idols. Why should I die now . . . now, when the pagans triumph over Your people?*

It's not fair! If I die now, the people will turn from You. They will have no one to lead them. And after that, Yahweh, how could You ever protect them? You couldn't. The Assyrians would be victorious, and Jerusalem would be trodden under the feet of the Gentiles. Your people will be scattered among the nations to languish—to disappear from the earth.

Hezekiah begged Yahweh to reconsider, to grant him a little more life to see the crisis through to a satisfactory conclusion. *Please let me see the victory. Let me witness You triumph over Your foes—and Judah free from tyranny!*

As the king pleaded his cause from his bedchamber, Isaiah crossed the royal gardens toward his humble home, still trembling over the message he had delivered. The prophet thought he would never counsel Hezekiah again.

But as Isaiah approached the palace gate a voice stopped him. "Return to the king," it commanded. "He has prayed for healing, and his prayer is heard. Take him another message."

With a smile on his face, Isaiah quickly retraced his steps. The surgeons, still huddling outside the bedchamber door, did not see the prophet pass them into the room.

Absorbed in his prayer, Hezekiah did not realize that anyone had entered. The touch of the prophet's hand gave his first indication of another person's presence. Halting his prayer in mid sentence, he turned and gazed into Isaiah's eyes. Instantly his agony changed to joy. His prayer had been answered! He knew it even before Isaiah spoke.

"Yahweh has heard you, Hezekiah," the prophet smiled,

"and has granted you more time. You will have 15 more years. The Lord also promised that Jerusalem will not fall to Sennacherib. He will hear a rumor and return to his own land without capturing the city. As a sign that this message is true, you will be well enough to pray in the Temple on the day after tomorrow."

"The news is better than I hoped for," the king exclaimed. "I asked for healing, but Yahweh is giving me 15 years. I asked for Jerusalem's safety, and Yahweh promises that the Assyrian will not conquer the city. Can it be true? How can I know that Yahweh has spoken—that this message is not merely wishful thinking on your part?"

"This is not simply my desire for you. Yahweh has decreed it. It will happen exactly as I have revealed it to you. To demonstrate that it is truly from the Lord, why not ask for a sign?" Isaiah strolled to the window and studied the garden outside. "Out there in the courtyard is the sundial erected by Ahaz." He stared at the step-like structure. "Would you like the sun's shadow to rise 10 degrees or to fall 10 degrees on it?"

Alert now, Hezekiah thought: *The sun always travels from east to west. To advance forward would be no great sign. But to shift backward . . . impossible.* "Have the shadow return 10 degrees. By this I will know that Yahweh has indeed spoken."

Isaiah's strong arms helped Hezekiah to the courtyard to see the sundial of Ahaz. Quickly the king noted the steps to which the shadow pointed and settled himself on a bench to wait. Within minutes the shadow began to slide in the wrong direction: one degree . . . two degrees . . . three degrees, four degrees. For 40 minutes Hezekiah forgot his pain as he gazed at the shadow crawling the wrong way—10 full degrees! A small crowd of court officials and servants gathered in the garden. "I know I asked for this sign," Hezekiah whispered, "yet it seems impossible! But here it is: The sun has moved backward 10 degrees!"

The Sign in the Sundial

How could it be? Hezekiah and his friends knew only that it had actually happened. Astrologers as far away as Babylon also witnessed the miracle. "Now I believe the message, Isaiah. Yahweh has given me a sign that is impossible to fake."

Returning to his bed, Hezekiah rested much easier. He did not know how God would heal him, but he knew it would be done.

By now the surgeons had returned, having decided what they would do. But what they now saw baffled them. They had left a despondent king on the verge of death. When they came back they found a joyful Hezekiah sitting on the edge of his bed, laughing and talking with a prophet whom they remembered leaving the palace an hour before. What did it all mean?

Isaiah explained that God had promised to heal Hezekiah. Instructing them to place a plaster of figs on the boil, he said, "If you do this, the king will soon be well."

The medical men reacted with horror. "Why, what does a prophet know about medicine?" Yet Isaiah showed such confidence that their resistance was fruitless. The king asked them to follow his instruction, and they did.

Within hours the king could eat with his son Manasseh and exchange pleasantries with his servants. He looked completely changed.

Two days later Hezekiah walked without aid to the Temple. His heart burst with love for God, who had saved him from death. Somehow, he told himself, he must help his people to know Yahweh. He must lead them to believe that Yahweh would save them from all their enemies. But how could they understand the events of the past months and still trust in Him?

As he entered the Temple Hezekiah's thoughts slipped into poetry. His heart swelled with joy until he could restrain himself no longer, and he had to shout his praise to Yahweh,

Siege at the Gates

his Savior. His words burst forth, full of melody:

> "I said: In the noon of my life
> I have to depart
> for the gates of Sheol,
> I am deprived of the rest of my years.

> "I said: I shall never see Yahweh again
> in the land of the living,
> never again look on any man
> of those who inhabit the earth.

> "My tent is pulled up, and thrown away
> like the tent of a shepherd;
> like a weaver you roll up my life
> to cut it from the loom.

> "From dawn to night you are compassing my end,
> I cry aloud until the morning;
> like a lion he crushes all my bones,
> from dawn to night you are compassing my end.

> "I am twittering like a swallow,
> I am moaning like a dove,
> my eyes turn to the heights,
> take care of me, be my safeguard.

> "What can I say? Of what can I speak to him?
> It is he who is at work;
> I will give glory to you all the years of my life
> for my sufferings.

> "Lord, my heart will live for you,
> my spirit will live for you alone.

You will cure me and give me life,
  my suffering will turn to health.

"It is you who have kept my soul
  from the pit of nothingness,
  you have thrust all my sins
  behind your back.

"For Sheol does not praise you,
  Death does not extol you;
  those who go down to the pit do not go on trusting
  in your faithfulness.

"The living, the living are the ones who praise you,
  as I do today.
  Fathers tell their sons
  about your faithfulness.

"Yahweh, come to my help
  and we will make our harps resound
  all the days of our life
  in front of the Temple of Yahweh."
                    —(Isa. 38:9-20, Jerusalem)

Chapter 13

Bird in a Cage

The only sign of the boil that nearly ended Hezekiah's life was the scar of a fast-healing wound. Buoyed by the promise that his life had been extended 15 years, he felt strong and confident. Yahweh had also assured him that the Assyrians would not destroy Jerusalem.

At first he eagerly waited for his envoys to return from Lachish. Then he began to fret. "I haven't heard from them for almost a week," he said one day.

"But, your Majesty," a servant reminded him, "the pack train and the Assyrian protocol would lengthen the normal travel time."

"You're right," the king reluctantly conceded. "And I couldn't expect anyone to bring messages back." The Judahite monarch paced in his chambers. "I guess we'll just have to wait."

Rumors soon circulated that Lachish had fallen, with thousands now tramping the dreary miles to Assyria. But Hezekiah hoped that what he heard was not true. "I trust my ambassadors were in time to prevent Sennacherib's armies from breaking through the wall." He fingered his signet ring. "And I hope my family is still safe within the royal retreat."

"Are they all right, Father?" Manasseh asked daily about his sisters and their mothers. "When can they come home? Do they have toys to play with? Do they have enough to eat?"

Hezekiah consoled the 7-year-old child as best he could, concealing his own concern for his family's safety. And yet his nagging conscience goaded him: Why didn't I keep them here? Constantly he pleaded with God for their safety.

Word of the envoys' return reached the palace before they did. The news was not encouraging. When they appeared in court, every fear that Hezekiah had harbored proved true. Shebna and his aides had torn their clothes and put ashes on their heads—an ancient sign of mourning. Lachish was no more!

And they had brought even worse tidings. "The Assyrians will not release any of the captives," Shebna reported. "They also refuse to end the war, even though they took our money. In fact, instead of stopping the invasion, Sennacherib demands unconditional surrender. If we don't, he will destroy Jerusalem."

"Even now," Eliakim added, "his armies march toward us. Any day they will encamp around the city."

Hezekiah refused to panic at the news, and he showed no fear of the attack on Jerusalem. Instead he smiled as though he knew something they did not—that the Assyrians would not, could not, conquer the capital.

The king summoned Judah's leaders to the Temple. "I want them to know of Assyria's plans and of Yahweh's promises." Then turning to Shebna and his aides he expressed concern for their health. "You have finished a hazardous mission and must be weary. Your families will rejoice to see you alive and well." He placed his hand on the steward's shoulder. "Why not go home, bathe, and get some rest? Don't fear. The enemy will not overcome Jerusalem. Yahweh has promised to spare His city."

The men felt strangely encouraged as they hurried home. Their journey had been arduous. The sight of a city in ruins, surrounded by corpses, had sickened them. They had recoiled from the execution of Lachish's elders and had watched in horror as the Assyrians marched others off to a foreign land. But the walls of Jerusalem comforted them.

"Everything will be all right now," Eliakim said as the men separated. "I'm sure of it. His majesty the king just told us that Yahweh will save our city."

"I hope so," Shebna replied slowly.

Hezekiah went to the Temple. On the way he paused to speak to the knots of worried citizens of Jerusalem who wondered what the future held. When he entered the Temple, he saw that most of the elders had already arrived.

"I wanted you to know the news firsthand," he explained. "Sennacherib spelled out his terms of truce, and we complied with them. But now he has double-crossed us." A murmur spread through the group. "He has taken our money but refuses to quit the war. At this moment he marches toward Jerusalem."

Tense voices expressed their alarm. But the king displayed no fear. "Everyone knows that I have recovered from a boil that nearly took my life. Just two days ago I celebrated the miracle of healing by worshipping here at the Temple. When Yahweh promised to heal, He also said that the Assyrians will not destroy Jerusalem. 'They will hear a rumor,' says Yahweh, 'that will cause them to hurry home.'"

Cries of "Hallelujah!" rose from several quarters. Hezekiah motioned for silence.

"We must repent of our sins so that Yahweh will be able to work in our behalf. We must pray for complete deliverance. We must covenant with God to remain true to Him no matter what may happen. If we do this, Yahweh will overcome the enemy."

As the king spoke, the watchman on the southwest corner of the city wall announced that the Assyrian forces were in sight.

Hezekiah hurried to the wall, wanting to see for himself. On the way he passed Shebna, wildly driving his chariot toward his tomb for a last look. The king shook his head as he climbed the steps to the watchman's tower. The palace steward must be crazy to leave the walls to inspect his tomb, he told himself. If he kept that up he would never use it. The official's behavior had raised serious doubts in the king's mind. Perhaps he should replace him. But there was no time for that now.

The watchmen greeted Hezekiah with alarm. Anyone on the wall was in danger when an enemy approached. But the king assured them that he would stay only a few minutes.

The sentries interpreted the scene for him. Thousands of armed soldiers swarmed over the distant hill. They accompanied countless wagons loaded with supplies, as well as hundreds of chariots—some bearing officers, others fitted for battle—drawn by the most beautiful horses the king had ever seen. The sight of such an army sent conflicting chills of admiration and fear through his heart. "No wonder every nation fears and flees so formidable a foe," he whispered to himself.

He remained on the wall as long as he dared. The forward troops soon reached arrow-shot range, and still more troops topped the ridge in the distance. Since the enemy soldiers presented a threat to his safety, Hezekiah retreated to a shelter at the base of the wall while the watchmen relayed the situation to him. None of the enemy had so far shot at those on the wall. The city's defenders held their arrows too. Quickly the enemy surrounded the city . . . and still more soldiers poured over the ridge.

The Assyrians established camps all around the city, posting guards, building fires, distributing food rations, and settling in for a long siege. A watchman spotted the royal Assyrian chariot passing the columns still marching down the ridge. It climbed the Mount of Olives, an excellent vantage point from which to observe the campaign. Messengers repeatedly overtook the chariot. The king's bodyguard erected the royal tent, and Sennacherib disappeared into it.

As daylight waned, a strange truce continued. While the people of Jerusalem watched, the Assyrians continued their siege preparations. At the same time thousands of workers transported weapons from the city's warehouses to the walls. Soldiers and civilians—all curious to see—crowded the turrets and walkways.

The sun melted into the hills, and long shadows draped a purple landscape. The sky turned deep velvet. Countless campfires flickered on the hills. Distant ridges sparkled with beacons that blended with the sky, making it difficult to determine where the fires ended and the stars began.

The night passed, and the campfires burned low. Dawn brought new activity, but different from that expected by the people of Jerusalem. Instead of showering the defenders on the walls with cascades of arrows, the Assyrians constructed siege machines. Streams of soldiers hacked down every tree around the city or hauled dirt and rocks to within a stone's throw of the wall for making ramps.

A messenger approached the main gate with a note for Hezekiah. Not desiring to risk opening the main gate, the guards lowered a basket. Hezekiah marveled that it was written in Hebrew. "You can see that you are badly outnumbered," it announced. "If you refuse to surrender, we will break down your walls, rape your women, kill your men, and carry every living thing into captivity. And you, Hezekiah, will not escape alive. But if you care for your life and for your people, you will surrender without a fight. We will transport all the people to peaceful lands, where they can enjoy pleasant lives, but none of the people will be slain."

"What kind of offer is this?" Hezekiah recoiled. "How can that pagan presume to bargain for the lives of God's people?" His anger flared. "Let Yahweh fight for us," he shouted. "I will not surrender Jerusalem to a Gentile king.

Yahweh has promised salvation. I will wait for Him to act."

It surprised Sennacherib to receive an answer so soon. He had expected Hezekiah at least to call his council for their advice. But Sennacherib's messenger had quickly returned with the reply, which made the Assyrian explode when he read the one-word challenge to his authority: "No!"

"How can Hezekiah be so stupid?" he roared. "Does he think he can hold out against me? Will he put his people through torture just to save face?"

After sending another threatening letter to the Judahite king, the Assyrian monarch also ordered his troops to begin the siege. "I will give that rebel something for him to meditate on," he hissed.

But the Assyrian forces never had a chance to go into action. As Sennacherib's messenger passed the word to the soldiers, another courier galloped on a sweat-frothed steed with reports from Babylon. The dispatch enraged Sennacherib. The Elamites had rebelled. "They have marched into Babylon," the dispatch stated, "driving out your troops. They crowned Merodach-baladan king of Babylon. Now they march toward Nineveh. Our armies are unable to hold them back and request that Sennacherib join them to save the city."

Sennacherib turned white with fury, and streaks of red climbed up his neck. "For months I have destroyed every ally of Hezekiah," he fumed. "I have left that Jew defenseless. But now that I have him shut up like a bird in a cage, this happens!" He slammed his fist into the palm of his hand. "If I had only two more months! If I could destroy Jerusalem now, I'd never be troubled with these pesky people again!"

For a moment he teetered in indecision. Then he realized that his empire was about to fall to the powerful Elamites, and he jerked back to reality. "Delay could be fatal!" he exclaimed to his officers. "We must leave immediately."

"But I must intimidate Hezekiah before I leave," he decided. So sending his messenger to the wall again, he delivered one last letter. It demanded the immediate release of Padi, former king of Ekron, and insisted that Judah deliver the taxes for the next year to Nineveh within the month. "If you meet these two conditions," the note stated, "the Assyrians will leave at once."

Hezekiah saw the hand of Yahweh in it, though others felt suspicious at the sudden turn of moods. The Assyrian ruler had not mentioned the Elamite revolt, yet Hezekiah knew that some rumor had frightened him, or he would never have offered such mild terms. "Yahweh has provided a way out," he explained to Shebna. "I will accept it."

When the royal messenger appeared atop the wall, he did not stand alone. Padi accompanied him. Within minutes the men on the wall rigged a basket to lower the former Philistine ruler to the valley floor. The king of Ekron bore in his hand Hezekiah's reply. "The tax, for which the great king asked, will be sent to Nineveh as requested."

Still disappointed at his failure, Sennacherib ordered his forces to break camp. His men left in haste, mostly riding in carts or on the backs of horses—two to each animal—and some in the battle chariots.

As the last of the Assyrians passed out of sight to the north, a cheer resounded from the soldiers on the wall and echoed from the people. A multitude of voices shouted their thanks to Yahweh and to King Hezekiah for deliverance from the enemy.

Chapter 14

A Time for Tears

For the first time in months the people of Judah could move about without danger from marauding soldiers. Hezekiah dispatched scouts to observe the Assyrian retreat. They soon returned, reporting, "The enemy has crossed the border. They seem in haste to get somewhere. We asked some shepherds if they had heard anything."

"What did they say?" the king asked eagerly.

"They say the rumor is that Elam has attacked Assyria."

The chaos they saw everywhere saddened the refugees as they left Jerusalem for their homes. Every village lay in shambles. The enemy had either harvested or burned any crops ready for harvest. The invaders had taken everything of value to Assyria or destroyed it.

The most heartbreaking thing of all was the utter lack of human life. Most all of their friends and families outside the Jerusalem wall were gone. The Assyrians had either killed or deported nearly every living thing.

In every village travelers could see the few haggard survivors sifting through the ruins of their former homes. Others wandered aimlessly or sat on stones that had been door thresholds or leaned in exhaustion against nearby rocks, staring into space. Occasionally an individual, a small family, or a child who had managed to escape by hiding in a cave, returned to the ruined village. The cruelty they had witnessed was unimaginable. From their caves they had watched their friends murdered or taken captive.

Siege at the Gates

The worst part was burying all the bodies. The warring Assyrians did not honor the dead. When people died, the invaders simply left them where they had fallen. They abandoned even their own soldiers to rot. The stench of decomposition permeated the land.

Hezekiah no longer feared for his kingdom, but now he agonized over his personal loss. Save for Hephzibah and Manasseh, he had sent all his family to Lachish. Now Lachish was no more, and his family had disappeared. "Where are my wives and children?" he asked everyone. But no one seemed to know.

A group of soldiers returned from Lachish with their report. "Have you found any trace of my wives or children?" he pleaded. The men had witnessed scenes that no human could forget—a city in ruins, filled with corpses. When they hesitated too long in answering, he demanded irritably, "What did you find?"

"Your majesty," the captain replied slowly, "we searched through the ruins, as you asked. We found the remains of the royal retreat. There were bodies of Assyrian and Jewish soldiers everywhere."

"My family!" the king shouted. "Did you find my family?"

"No." The soldier almost choked. "We found no trace that any of them died in or around the city. We must assume they were taken captive."

Exhausted, the king sank back. Filled with guilt and bitterness, he grieved his loss. Finally he managed to speak. "Thank you for your work. You may go."

Retiring to his chambers, he busied himself with matters of state, hoping to ease his mind. But it was impossible. Still he had been there only a few minutes when Shebna's secretary entered.

"Ah, Eliakim." Hezekiah managed to smile. He had always felt warmly toward this man. The king understood why people referred to him as their father—not because of his age, for the man was still relatively young. But Eliakim treated everyone graciously. "And what," asked the king, "can I do for you today?"

The official bowed in respect. "To be in your presence is all that I could desire."

The king had heard the insincere phrase thousands of times, but Eliakim meant every word. The king liked him. "You may stay as long as you like, my friend." Hezekiah seldom used that word. "But you must have some reason for coming today."

"Yes, your majesty." Eliakim paused. "I have heard that you desire to know the fate of your family."

"Do you know anything about them?" Hezekiah tensed.

"Yes," the secretary hesitated, "but I thought you already knew."

"Knew!" the king exploded. "I wish I knew! I've searched for someone to give me even a drop of information." Embarrassed at having lashed out at so close a friend, Hezekiah forced himself to calm down. "I just never thought of asking you. Tell me, Eliakim . . . what has happened to them?"

The secretary's lip trembled, and he glanced away from his master's eyes. "They are in Nineveh," he whispered. "Sennacherib will put them into his harem."

The horror etched on the king's features frightened Eliakim. The king buried his head in his hands. To him such captivity was worse than death. For nearly an hour he sobbed, with Eliakim's hand on his shoulder to comfort him. Finally Hezekiah managed to ask, "Where did you learn this?"

"Sennacherib told us during our second visit."

"Your second visit? That was weeks ago! Why didn't you say something before this?"

"I thought Shebna briefed you on our conference with the Assyrian ruler."

"He did." Hezekiah's face hardened. "But he didn't say a word about my family!"

A tension-filled silence settled over the chamber. Hezekiah mentally reviewed his doubts about the steward: Shebna's preoccupation with his tomb; his chariot, designed to outrival the royal one; his sometimes questionable dealings. And now his seemingly deliberate suppression of knowledge regarding the fate of the king's family. It was too much.

"I'm afraid Shebna has robbed his own tomb," the king announced. "I shall ask him to resign. And you, Eliakim . . ." A smile broke over his face. "You shall be my new steward."

"Me? Why, I'm only a scribe! Joah would do far better than—"

"No, Eliakim. I can think of no one who would do better." Instantly Hezekiah realized that he had embarrassed the gentle man. "Now say nothing about this. I'll see to it."

When the king approached Shebna about the matter, the official—angry and embarrassed—lashed out at his ruler while denying the facts. But he could not change Hezekiah's mind and departed the palace a lowly scribe assigned to work for his former secretary.

Sennacherib had been gone only a few weeks when envoys came to Hezekiah from Babylon. The men were ambassadors of Merodach-baladan, the former client king of the Assyrians. Greeting Hezekiah in his own language, they brought the best wishes of Merodach-baladan and congratulated the king on his recovery from the recent illness. Perhaps, they said, the king could explain to them, for the benefit of their leader, how the sun came to travel 10 degrees backward through the sky?

"Rumors in Babylon say that Yahweh caused the sun to return as a sign that you would be healed." The ambassadors felt as though they were on the verge of a great discovery.

"Can Yahweh be greater than the gods of Babylon?" Their interest was unmistakable, though they feared to blaspheme their own deities.

"Shamash—the sun—has never been known to retreat," they continued. "He always advances from east to west. But now he has retreated." A dramatic pause electrified the throne room. "Did Yahweh cause our deity to retreat? Tell us. We must report to Merodach-baladan."

The king marveled that Babylon would send ambassadors to Judah. Sennacherib had all but destroyed his country after Hezekiah's supposed Palestinian friends abandoned him. But Babylon asked him about his God! The thought flattered Hezekiah, but he could think of nothing to say to them.

Then something snapped within his mind. Perhaps he desired an alliance with Babylon to frustrate any future attack from Assyria. The Babylonian ruler had rebelled against his Assyrian overlord and now ruled independently. He was a powerful individual. Perhaps he could be useful to Hezekiah. For whatever reason, instead of explaining Yahweh's greatness in order to win converts to the true God, the Judahite king gave his visitors a tour of Jerusalem.

The taxes to Sennacherib had drained the silver and gold from the palace and Temple treasuries, but it had not touched the private fortunes of the wealthy merchants or the crown jewels of the palace. Hezekiah's recent taxes had already brought revenues into his treasury for sending on to Assyria. Jerusalem's ornate buildings surpassed those of many other cities. Babylon was proverbial for its splendor, but the beauty and wealth they saw impressed the ambassadors.

"It's a marvel that these riches still exist," one of them remarked as they entered their guest suite. "Remember, Sennacherib spent 12 months in Palestine removing every valuable object."

"That's true," another commented. "But did you notice

the artistic talents these people have?" He thought of the many objects he had seen that day. "We have little in Babylon, or in Elam, to compare with them."

"You're right. If we could only have these craftsmen in our country." He stopped, but his implications were obvious to his friends.

Hezekiah had hoped to impress the ambassadors with the strength and riches of Jerusalem. Maybe, he reasoned, Merodach-baladan would ally with him. The Babylonian ruler would not be like those cowards in Palestine. The king's eyes narrowed as he worked through his plan. If he had support like that in the east, he could also accomplish what Yahweh had done. He smiled to himself. Then he could rebel against Assyria and . . . and when Sennacherib came he could call on Babylon for help. Merodach-baladan would then march on Nineveh, and the Assyrians would leave Judah alone.

Hezekiah paced in his private chambers. Perhaps it might even be possible to work from both sides to destroy Assyria. The king grinned at his scheme.

As a result, he showed his guests more wealth and armaments until they had seen all. They reviewed his armies and toured his food and weapons storehouses, his defense systems, and his water tunnel. He treated them to the best food and wine and entertained them with Jerusalem's finest dancers and musicians. When he had done his best, he sent them off with gracious greetings for their king.

When the Babylonian envoys had arrived in Jerusalem, they had asked about the miracle of Hezekiah's healing and the phenomenon of the retreating sun. They had longed to know of Yahweh. But they learned nothing of Him. Instead, they left with the dazzle of riches in their eyes. They carried no answer at all to the riddle of the healing or of the movement of the shadow cast by the sundial. Their only message for Merodach-baladan was, "If we could only have Judah's wealth, our country would far surpass any nation in the world."

Hezekiah still congratulated himself on the way he treated his guests when Isaiah entered his chambers without introduction. The prophet often did that, and the king thought nothing of it. Casually, Isaiah asked, "Who were those men, and what did they say?"

"They were ambassadors from Babylon. Didn't you know that?"

"What did they see in your house, Hezekiah?" The old man's voice had an ominous ring.

Suddenly Hezekiah felt somewhat uneasy. "Why everything," he answered. "I showed them all my riches, my armies, my defenses. There is nothing among my treasures that I didn't reveal."

The king's face paled as he realized what he had done. He had never thought that their ruler would covet such things for himself. Horror written on his face, he slumped into a chair.

Isaiah dreaded the message he must give, knowing it would hurt, but he did not refrain. Stepping to the side of the king, he placed his hand on the royal shoulder. "Hear the word of Yahweh," he began and then hesitated. Hezekiah motioned for him to continue. "The days will come when everything in your house will be carried to Babylon. Nothing shall be left, says Yahweh."

Although Isaiah paused, the king knew that he hadn't finished. "What else has God said?" he whispered.

"They shall take away your descendants to be slaves in the palace of the king of Babylon."

Terror seized Hezekiah. He had spent his life leading his people back to Yahweh so they could have freedom from their enemies. But now he had betrayed them. "I have sinned!" he exclaimed, sweat beading on his brow. His head sank into his hands, and he sobbed, a heartbroken man. "How can Yahweh forgive me for betraying Him and His people?"

Isaiah remained while Hezekiah mourned his sin, begging Yahweh for forgiveness and mercy. At last the king regained his composure and realized that his friend still waited by his side. Hezekiah pleaded for Isaiah to intercede in his behalf.

Gazing out the window as though lost in thought, the prophet remained silent. Then, under the inspiration of God's Holy Spirit, he said, "You have repented with tears, Hezekiah. The judgment will not come during your life. Jerusalem and all of Judah will be taken by the king of Babylon. But you will not see it happen."

The king quietly thanked him. He longed to recall his mindless acts, but sadly, that could not be. At least he would not see the outcome of his deed, but his heart grieved that he had cursed future generations. "Sin is always like that," he mused aloud. "Every sin brings trouble—not only upon ourselves but upon innocent people who have had nothing to do with it."

"That's true," Isaiah murmured.

"Thanks be to Yahweh." The king's eyes still melted into pools of tears. " 'The Lord is merciful and gracious.' "

The prophet recognized the words of the psalm and joined in unison with his royal friend. " 'Neither will he keep his anger for ever.' "

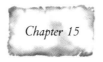
Chapter 15

So Little Time

In the years following his invasion of Judah, Sennacherib focused his attention on Babylonia and Elam, in the process destroying the city of Babylon. "Sennacherib is too busy to worry about us," Hezekiah told Eliakim one day. "I doubt he'll have time to notice a missing tribute payment."

"I don't know," Eliakim replied carefully, troubled. "He has many people keeping account of the taxes." The new steward stared at his sandals. "I wouldn't count on his overlooking a thing like that."

"Come, Eliakim. You're too cautious. Judah needs that money to rebuild. If that menace returns, we'll be ready for him." The king felt pleased with his decision.

However, Isaiah counseled against it. "'Woe to them that . . . trust in chariots . . . and in horsemen, because they are very strong; but they look not unto the Holy One of Israel.'"

"But, Isaiah," Hezekiah objected. "I do trust in Yahweh. You know yourself that I have led this people to follow Him as no other king since Asa."

"That's true. But you still rely on alliances and the strength of fortifications and armies. You must learn to put your confidence in Yahweh alone. He will protect you from all your enemies. But without Him, you will be helpless before a band of desert robbers."

Hezekiah said he appreciated the prophet's concern but felt he was already following his counsel. Sennacherib had failed to capture Jerusalem the first time, and the king believed he would still be unable to take it if he returned. Deep inside, the king expected Yahweh to protect the city no matter what happened.

But at the same time the ruler prepared for the sure return of Assyrian forces when they would eventually finish their Babylonian campaign.

The wall around Jerusalem had been greatly strengthened. But now new proposals seemed necessary. "Our engineers warn us that we are still vulnerable to Assyrian attack," Hezekiah explained. "Millo—the fortress of David—has a strong wall. But it will be easily breached. The ground outside the wall is level there." He showed them plans drawn by his engineers.

The chief engineer interpreted the drawings. "We should build a second wall around the city. This will make it doubly difficult for an enemy to break into Jerusalem. Between the walls"—he stabbed his finger at the drawing—"we plan for a dry moat. Anyone who breaks through the first wall will find themselves in a low gully with another wall still to breach."

"Looks like that would be impossible for them to do," Joah interrupted.

"Very nearly so," the engineer replied. "You'll notice the strengthened fortress at Millo. The double walls and the dry moat will make it impossible for the enemy to break through there."

"I like the idea of the second wall," Shebna nodded, still studying the plans. "It will rule out a quick breakthrough into the city, like the Assyrians did at Lachish."

Silence suddenly fell over the room at the mention of Lachish. But Hezekiah appeared not to notice. "The deep ditch between the walls will make it difficult for the Assyrians to use battering rams on the inner wall," he observed.

The elders approved the concept, and a messenger carried orders to the laborers to begin work.

"I was embarrassed at the way our troops acted during the last invasion." The king frowned. "Refusal to fight the enemy is cowardly, but refusing help to fellow countrymen and women is criminal." He remembered his pleas for the army to save the country. "I believe"—he rested both his fists on the table—"I believe we need an investigation. Which of our officers led in that demoralizing affair?" His eyes narrowed to slits. "Those who were guilty must be replaced. We cannot let it happen again."

Construction of the new city walls took top priority. In order to make a place for the walls—and to provide easily accessible building materials—the king's men made a list of all houses sitting next to the construction site. They would dismantle some of the older buildings and relocate the people. But despite all the activity, no one doubted the strength of the Assyrians. They realized that in spite of the walls, fortresses, and moats, the Assyrians would conquer Jerusalem—unless Yahweh intervened.

But regardless they must still prepare for the eventual siege. Surely Yahweh expected them to take some steps to protect themselves. Then they were to trust in Him to save them when they could no longer help themselves.

Though Isaiah pleaded with Hezekiah not to break away from Assyria, the king refused to listen. He had determined to leave Judah free from foreign rule when he died. The cost would be high, but he felt that loyalty to his nation, and to his God, demanded no less than an all-out campaign for freedom.

"And now is the time," he mumbled aloud as he prepared for bed one night. The oil lamp beside his bed cast grotesque shadows across his bearded face.

"The time for what?" Hephzibah asked, already curled up facing the wall.

The king stared for a moment into a dark corner of the room. "Now is the time to be free from Assyria, because . . ."

125

He hesitated to hear the words, but knew that he must speak them. "Because for me, time is running out."

The king pulled a blanket up under his beard, his mind astir with conflicting emotions. For a long time he listened to the rhythmic breathing of his wife. Finally, not long before dawn, he drifted into troubled sleep. But even his dreams reminded him . . . that time was running out . . . so much to do . . . so little time . . . so . . . little . . .

Chapter 16

The Wolf and the Fold

The army scout spurred his Egyptian mare through the crowded streets of Jerusalem, brushing people aside. In his haste he toppled a stack of woven baskets. A woman lost her balance, dropping the full water pot from her head and leaving a thousand wet fragments of pottery on the ground. Angry cries and anxious glances followed the soldier as he hurried to the palace. The expression on his face, his urgency, caused many to turn and follow him. They sensed that he bore news of national importance.

The guards quickly opened the palace gates, and the rider galloped the last few hundred cubits. Dismounting in a single bound, he hurried into the palace, not waiting for the herald to announce his arrival.

Hezekiah looked up from a planning session with his counselors.

"I beg your pardon for entering unannounced, your majesty," the rider said. Fear filled his eyes. "I have hurried to tell you that Sennacherib is approaching."

Whispers rustled in the room, and anxious glances shot in every direction as the messenger continued. "Even now he nears our borders and will be in position to attack within a few days."

For several seconds everyone remained silent. At last Eliakim found his voice. "Where are they now?"

"Near the borders of Tyre and Sidon, on the King's

Highway. We expect that they will go by the way of the Great Sea."

"Are they traveling quickly?" Shebna asked.

"Not as fast as they left Jerusalem last time. But they move at a rapid pace."

"How many men would you judge them to have?" Hezekiah inquired.

"That's hard to say." The scout had a distant look in his eye. "I stood on a hill as they passed. Their soldiers, horses, and wagons overflowed the road into the fields for many cubits." Then he paused as though in a trance. "I watched until the front lines marched over the horizon toward the south . . . and still . . . still they came over the edge of the earth from the north. They are beyond counting."

"Is there anything else?" Eliakim persisted.

"No. What will we do? They'll carry us away to Nineveh!"

"Now, now, my son." Eliakim's voice soothed like that of a father calming his child during a thunderstorm. "Come with me. You must be tired and hungry. Everything will be all right. . . ." His voice trailed off as he led the frightened messenger out of the council chamber.

None of the elders doubted Sennacherib's intentions. He planned to crush Jerusalem out of existence. "I suppose he is still angry he didn't get us 10 years ago," Shebna mumbled.

"Yes," Joah added, "and it looks as if he plans to do it this time . . . like a wolf descending upon a fold."

"But he won't destroy our fold if we trust in Yahweh." Hezekiah had remained unaffected by the despair. "Come now. We must plan our actions." His calm soon revived the group.

"We need to warn our people," Joah said. "They'll need time to retreat into the walled cities."

"That's already being done," Eliakim stated as he returned to the room. "The royal messenger service will get the word to every town in Judah by nightfall."

Hezekiah nodded. "Good. Now let's get on with our plans."

It required only a few hours for the news to reach the farthest villages. Few seemed surprised, for all had expected the Assyrians to return. No one panicked. They packed the few valuables they could carry and headed for safety.

And safety meant only one thing: Jerusalem. The capital was the only city to survive the previous invasion. The entire adult population owed their existence to the fact that they had been in Jerusalem when Sennacherib had invaded before. They felt that their only hope this time was to flee into the holy city.

People arrived in Jerusalem at first in small groups, then in ever-increasing numbers. From early morning until late night they poured in by the thousands. Many stayed with friends. Others camped in the streets or any available open space. Fugitives flooded into the city until the 86-acre fortress bulged with men, women, and children, besides all the animals.

The construction crews had toiled to strengthen Judah's walled cities. And yet people took no chances. Even Lachish and Libnah, the strongest fortifications outside Jerusalem, were now empty except for the armed troops stationed there. A few brave individuals remained, but most people had decided that Jerusalem was their only hope.

Hezekiah observed the influx of fugitives with concern. "With this mass of people," he commented to Eliakim, "and the Assyrians due to arrive any time, I'm afraid we don't have enough food. And threat of disease breaking out in such crowded circumstances increases every day."

"You may be right," the steward said. "We provided each city with food for the people there. But they're all coming here."

"And we don't have time to transfer the supplies to Jerusalem."

"Nor room, either." Joah had just stepped in.

"Joah!" The king seemed pleased to see his recorder. "I was just going to send for you." The monarch looked across the city. "How many people are in Jerusalem now?"

The official gave an estimate, and Hezekiah shook his head. "Do we have enough food and water?"

"That depends on how long the siege lasts."

"I know." The king glanced at him. "Suppose it lasts a year, Joah. Would we have enough?"

"No! That is . . . unless we cut the amount each person uses."

"That's what I wanted to know." The king made his decision. "So . . . we will ration the food."

The people chafed at first. They had been eating well for 10 years, and the cutback hurt. The authorities put a similar restriction on water. Overseers made sure that each family received its share—but no more. They placed a 24-hour guard at the Pool of Siloam and the reservoir, thus assuring that water coming through Hezekiah's tunnel would meet their needs during the months ahead.

The king was restless to know the position of the Assyrian troops. "There must be something we can do," he stormed to the council one day. "We mustn't just sit here like rats in a cage."

"Your Majesty, why not send an ambassador to Egypt?" Shebna suggested. "Perhaps they'll help us again."

"That's a good idea." Joah nodded his approval. "It was the only country to come to our aid last time."

"I don't know." Eliakim seemed a little cautious. "They got quite a beating then."

The recorder jumped to his feet. "But they have a new king now—Tirhakah the Nubian."

"And I hear he's a young man," Hezekiah offered. "I think he's only 19 or 20 years old. He would be more willing to face Sennacherib. This sounds better all the time."

"That's right. If anyone can defeat Sennacherib, Egypt can," Shebna concluded.

"It's worth a try," Joah insisted, sitting down again.

"Did I overhear you speaking about sending to Egypt for help?"

Hearing the voice, everyone turned to face Isaiah. The prophet's shocked expression paralyzed the council. For a moment he stood silently, almost in a trance, gazing at the men before him but seeing something else. After a long time his eyes focused, his muscles relaxed, and he spoke. "'Woe to the rebellious children,' saith Yahweh, 'that take counsel, but not of me; that trust in Pharaoh and stand in the shadow of Egypt.'" Isaiah paused and stared at them a moment. "The strength of Pharaoh shall be your shame, and trust in Egypt your confusion. For the Egyptians shall help in vain."

No one said anything after Isaiah abruptly left. At last Hezekiah broke the silence. "I love that man and dearly appreciate his counsel. We will put our trust in Yahweh. But I still believe we should send an ambassador to Egypt."

The counselors nodded wordlessly. Who could say what was right? After they departed, the king mused on the tactics of the Assyrians. He remembered how they had destroyed his allies first, leaving Judah with no one to help. Then, after crushing the rest of the nation, they had approached Jerusalem. "I'm sure they'll do the same this time," he said aloud. "But this time I have no allies. Sennacherib will attack me first."

With a frown he thought of Judah's prospects. The Assyrian king would have had no previous campaigns to tire his men and reduce their numbers. And there would be little chance that trouble elsewhere could erupt quickly enough to save Judah. If only Egypt were closer. If only he had sent the ambassador sooner.

The king chuckled at the thought of Isaiah's message. The prophet was right. He and his advisers were fooling themselves by requesting aid from Egypt. They could not count on that power. Their only hope lay in Yahweh. So in Yahweh they would trust.

Within a week of the first warning, Assyrian soldiers roamed Judah. Again Sennacherib sought to weaken Judah by attacking the smaller cities and towns first, leaving Jerusalem until last. The country crawled with troops who were raiding towns, burning crops, capturing livestock and killing what few people they could find.

"It doesn't matter," he told his officers when they commented about the deserted towns. "Soon we'll have Jerusalem, and all the people will be at our mercy."

"Or lack of it," one officer scowled.

Sennacherib exploded. "Watch it—I could have your head for that!"

The officer bowed in submission and turned away, furious but helpless. He would witness another bloodbath as the nation breathed its last. And like it or not, his only hope of personal survival lay in his participation in the affair.

With no opposition anywhere, it required but a few days for the Assyrians to reduce Judah to rubble. Meeting resistance in the large cities only, they left the fortresses untouched until they had destroyed the rest of the country. But soon only three cities remained: Lachish, Libnah, and Jerusalem.

Sennacherib gathered his army at Lachish. Remembering the battle plans of his previous trip, he was annoyed at the city's strengthened walls—far stronger than before. After leading his generals on a tour around the city as he planned the methods for capturing it, he decided, despite the thicker walls, to use the same tactics. "We will build ramps against the walls," he explained, "and use our battering rams and catapults. Then we'll tunnel under the wall right over there." He pointed to a spot near where they had dug their previous tunnel.

All of it would take time. But he had more troops than before, and they could accomplish the task in only a few weeks. In fact, speed was their best weapon. Sennacherib organized his army into shifts to continue the work day and night. The Assyrian ruler wanted to conquer Lachish and Libnah quickly so he could go to Jerusalem before anything hindered him from meeting his goal. He determined to completely destroy Judah and Hezekiah.

Daily the ramps grew against the walls. Work progressed nicely on the tunnel, too, and Sennacherib knew that the time drew near for the final push.

Perhaps . . . Sennacherib thought, *I can get Hezekiah to surrender Jerusalem without a fight.* He smiled at the idea. It was worth a try. First he discussed the plan with his chief cupbearer and high official, the Rabshakeh. More than just protecting the king from assassination by poison, he was also a man of great learning, speaking several languages fluently and often acting as an ambassador. His sensitive position made him a highly trusted person.

Sennacherib explained his plan. "I want you to take an army to Jerusalem." The Rabshakeh smiled as the king said, "Tell the Jews we want them to surrender Jerusalem without a fight. If they do, we will merely deport them. But if they won't . . ." He eyes hardened. "If they won't, there will be no more Jerusalem, and no more Jews."

"When shall I begin, your highness?"

"Right now! And don't speak merely to Hezekiah's envoys. Talk to the people on the wall . . . in their own language. Tell them what will happen if they don't surrender. You may even persuade them to rebel and hand over the king to us."

Siege at the Gates

Hezekiah summoned his nation's leaders. "We must encourage our people to trust in Yahweh," he urged. "Sennacherib will try everything to take our city. First he will attempt to persuade us to surrender; and if that fails, he will use force."

"If the people confess their sins and walk in God's laws, He will protect them—even against Assyria," Isaiah added.

The king then recalled how Yahweh had protected the city before. "You'll remember how Isaiah predicted that the enemy would hear a rumor and leave."

"I remember that very well," Shebna interrupted.

"You'll also remember that while Sennacherib's army encamped around our city they received word of the Babylonian rebellion. Yahweh protected us before, and He can do it again. If we make all things right with Him and trust in His power, He will save us."

The prophet held up his hand for attention. "Behold, Yahweh has said, 'If My people will not repent, then the Assyrians will carry them to Nineveh.'" A smile crossed his face. "The word which Yahweh gives me is: 'My people have repented; they are faithful to Me. They have listened to My prophet.' Therefore, 'the Assyrians will not shoot an arrow at Jerusalem. They have mounted to heaven in their haughtiness and have become bloody in their deeds. Yahweh will deal with them. They will know that He is God, the Creator.'"

Cheers filled the chamber, but Isaiah motioned for silence. "Yahweh will fight for this city. May the people remain true to Him. Stand still, and see the salvation of Yahweh, the Lord of hosts!"

Chapter 17

Minions in
the Fuller's Field

Sennacherib remained at Lachish while the Rabshakeh journeyed to Jerusalem. He took with him the Tartans—the Assyrian field marshals—a force large enough to begin a siege, and the Rabsaris—the king's chief eunuch. The 27-mile journey required two days because of the mountains, the narrow roads, and the thousands of men with their equipment. When they arrived, they found the gates closed and a large army spread along all of the outer walls.

"We can't talk with Hezekiah," the Rabsaris observed as they neared the city. "No Jew in their right mind would venture out here." He laughed at his own joke.

"We haven't come merely to see Hezekiah," the Rabshakeh replied. "But you know that he'll get the message."

The two officials pushed their way through the soldiers who had stopped just out of arrow-shot range of the wall. The chief Tartan joined them. "Well, Rabshakeh"—the field marshal looked tense—"I hope you can convince them to surrender." He studied the walls. "These are the strongest fortifications I've yet seen in Judah. It would take months to break through. Did you notice the double walls?" The officer drew a whistling breath through his teeth. "It would be death for my men to try to break through that second wall."

"Don't give up yet, Tartan," the Rabshakeh sneered. "If there's one thing I don't need, it's a cowardly general." The cupbearer turned to the Rabsaris, giving the Tartan a visible snub. "My, look at our audience." He pointed to the wall. "It seems that half the city has turned out to watch the parade." The two laughed while the general turned away in disgust, having never cared for high non-military officials. He got along better with his fighting men.

"If we can convince those people they can't win," the Rabshakeh said, "they might refuse to fight. They might even hand Hezekiah over to us."

"It's worth a try," the Rabsaris answered. "They'll save themselves a lot of bloodshed if they do."

As the Tartan spread his troops around the city to make the best show of force, the Rabshakeh looked for a suitable place to speak with the people on the wall. Finally he chose a level site along the road to the fuller's field.

The Assyrian didn't know the history of the spot, but the elders watching from the walls remembered it as the place where Isaiah gave his message of hope to Ahaz. At that time other armies had besieged Judah "Have no fear," Isaiah had told the king, "because of Israel and Syria. Yahweh says this: 'It shall not happen!'" And Assyria had destroyed the two nations. Now the Rabshakeh approached the same site, and the prophet again had promised salvation for Judah.

But the Rabshakeh knew nothing about it. He saw only a convenient place from which to fulfill his mission. Here by the highway of the fuller's field he could approach close enough to talk with the people.

"Oh, watchman!" the Rabshakeh called from the conduit of one of the pools by the road. "Fetch Hezekiah for me. I have a message for him."

It sounded more like taunting than a request for an audience with their ruler. "Who is this uncircumcised pagan," one soldier on the wall protested, "that he calls for the king as a man summons his dog?" The archer notched an arrow in his bowstring.

"Careful there, soldier," his leader cautioned. "We are not to shoot at them until the king orders it." Returning the arrow to its quiver, the frustrated soldier quietly observed the scene.

Hezekiah decided to stay off the wall. "My death," he explained to Eliakim, "would make Jerusalem an easy prey for them. No, you go, Eliakim. You will be safe. They wouldn't dare harm you. That would upset the people and spoil Sennacherib's plan."

Taking Shebna and Joah with him, the steward climbed the steep steps to the top of the wall. The Rabshakeh turned to the eunuch as the envoys appeared among the soldiers on the wall. "I see Hezekiah is intelligent."

"Yes," the other agreed. "I should have known better, but I pictured the king himself as possibly coming to meet us."

The cupbearer appeared disappointed. "It would have been nice to have embarrassed him personally." Approaching closer to the wall, he called over his shoulder, "I guess it doesn't really matter. Hezekiah will get the message soon enough."

"Thus speaks the great king of Assyria," the Rabshakeh began in Hebrew. "What makes you so confident? Do you think empty words are as good as military strength?" A murmur rustled through the crowd above him. "Who are you relying on, to dare to rebel against me? We know you rely on that broken reed Egypt, which pricks and pierces the hand of the man who leans on it. That is what Pharaoh is like to all who rely on him."

Shebna and Eliakim glanced at each other. "Do you think they captured our messenger?" Shebna whispered.

"I doubt it. He left several days before the Assyrians entered Judah."

"But how else could Rabshakeh speak so confidently?" Shebna was visibly worried.

"You may say to me: 'We rely on Yahweh our God,'"

Rabshakeh sneered, "but Hezekiah has suppressed His high places, saying to the people, 'In Jerusalem is the altar before which you must worship.'"

"How does he know that?" Joah whispered.

"The Assyrians have good spies," Eliakim answered.

"He's right about the high places. But he misunderstands the reasons. He doesn't know that those 'high places' were pagan shrines opposed to Yahweh. Hezekiah actually pleased the God that the Rabshakeh claims he annoyed. He's either confused, or else he's deliberately trying to confuse the people."

"Come, make a wager with the king of Assyria," the Assyrian cupbearer shouted to the silent walls. "I will give you 2,000 horses if you can find horsemen to ride them." He laughed to show how ridiculous the suggestion was. "How could you repulse a single weak Assyrian? And yet you rely on Egypt for chariots and horsemen." More laughter.

The insult came through loud and clear. The Jews had few horses in their army, a fact well known to the enemy. But the Rabshakeh claimed they couldn't even find men strong enough even to sit on horses.

Eliakim's face turned crimson. The Rabshakeh spoke in Hebrew so the crowds could understand every word. Most of what he said wasn't true at all and would undermine the people's morale for them to hear it from a foreigner.

Seeking to prevent trouble, Eliakim shouted to the Rabshakeh in Aramaic, the language of Assyrian commerce. "Please speak to your servants in Aramaic," he instructed him. "We understand it. Do not speak to us in Hebrew within earshot of the people."

Infuriated, the cupbearer refused to change.languages. Instead, he shouted louder and turned his attention from the envoys to the city's soldiers. "Do you think my lord sent me to speak to you? I was sent to speak to the doomed people on the walls."

Rabshakeh smiled at the embarrassment of the envoys. Now was the time to strike. Cupping his hands to his mouth, he shouted again, "Listen to the great king of Assyria. 'Do not let Hezekiah persuade you to trust in Yahweh by saying: "Yahweh is sure to save us from the power of Assyria." Do not listen to Hezekiah. The king of Assyria says this: 'Make peace with me, and every one of you will eat the fruit of his own vine and drink the water of his own cistern, until l deport you to a country like your own so you may not die but live.' Do not listen to Hezekiah when he says: 'Yahweh will save us.' Has any god of any nation saved his country from the power of Assyria? Where are the gods of Hamath and Arpad? Where are the gods of Sepharvaim, Hena, and Ivah? Where are the gods of Samaria? Tell me, which of the gods of any country have saved their people from my hands, and you think Yahweh is able to save Jerusalem?"

By exalting Assyrian power above Yahweh, the Assyrian unknowingly blasphemed the name of the great God who had created heaven and earth.

What a terrible day! Eliakim thought to himself. *And all those people hear these horrible things.* His face was so red that the Assyrian soldiers could see it even from a distance, but he remained silent, as did everyone else. Some feared Hezekiah's wrath. Others cringed at the challenge of the Rabshakeh. Still others recognized the lies and saw only a cruel man from a heartless nation.

Slowly Hezekiah's ambassadors retraced their steps to the king. Tears filled Eliakim's eyes as he realized that he must repeat the words to Hezekiah. In his grief he ripped his expensive robes to show his sorrow. Shebna and Joah followed his example. Then the trio halted beside a doorway where some woman had dumped ashes from her fire. Each took a handful of ashes and sprinkled it over his head—another traditional sign of mourning.

Siege at the Gates

Reluctantly they continued on their journey. At the palace they discovered that Hezekiah had already learned of Rabshakeh's blasphemy and needed to hear only the actual wording. He, too, tore his garments and mourned. Leaving his throne, he sat cross-legged on the floor, surrounded by his servants. "Today is a day of disgrace. May Yahweh hear the words of the Rabshakeh, and may He punish him for the words He has heard."

Sending the envoys to Isaiah, Hezekiah requested the prophet to pray for the people left in Judah. The elders rose slowly and trudged to the prophet's humble home. After some time they returned, cheered by what they had heard.

Hezekiah awaited their message. "Well, Eliakim?"

The steward smiled. "Isaiah says, 'Do not be afraid of the minions—the servants—of Sennacherib. I am going to send him back to his own country, and there I will kill him with a sword.'"

"Indeed!" Hezekiah exclaimed. "Yahweh will fight the battle for us."

Chapter 18

A Letter From Yahweh

When Eliakim, Shebna, and Joah left the walls, the Rabshakeh tried to get the attention of the people. "Your slave masters have turned their backs," he taunted. "We can talk together now about your future. If you follow Hezekiah and Yahweh, you're only going to cause yourself a lot of pain. You don't want that."

The people on the wall recognized that the cupbearer was talking down to them. The Assyrians believed the Jews to be of low intelligence. When they refused to answer, he persisted. "Hezekiah must be a self-centered man. He has rebelled against the great king and refused to send the taxes he promised. Probably he's been putting the money he gets from you into his own purse. And who's going to pay for his selfishness? You are . . . with your lives and those of your families."

Fierce anger tinged his voice as he waved at the army behind him. "These soldiers well know how to torture and kill. And that's why they're here. They have come to torture and kill you!"

Then the cupbearer changed his approach. "I can spare you this torture and death. None of you need suffer hunger for another day. If you follow my counsel, I guarantee we will go home. We will give you a better place to live than this rocky wilderness. What do you say to that?"

He paused for an answer, but none came. Not a person on the wall even whispered to their neighbor. "Why don't you answer me?" the Rabshakeh roared. "Don't you know that I have your lives in my hands? Turn Hezekiah over to me, and you will all go free. What do you say?"

Silence still cloaked the throngs on the wall.

"I cannot understand why they follow such a stupid king," he snapped to the Rabsaris. "It's obvious they can't resist our armies. But they're an obstinate bunch!"

Finally the two Assyrians made themselves comfortable under a tree, and the soldiers seated themselves on the hillsides around the city. Their numbers staggered the imagination, covering the hills like swarms of locusts. Impatiently they waited for Hezekiah to answer Rabshakeh.

The day waned, and the army pitched its tents. Still no word from Hezekiah. Night passed, a new day dawned, and yet no response came from the Jewish king. At last the cupbearer made a decision. "There's nothing more we can do here," he announced. "If Hezekiah is frightened, he will send messengers to Sennacherib as he did before. Let's return to Lachish."

The army had begun to form into ranks for the 27-mile march when a courier guided his mount through the men to the Rabshakeh.

"I have a message for you from the great king." The rider placed a leather pouch in the Rabshakeh's hand and dismounted.

The cupbearer slipped the roll of parchment from its pouch and unrolled it from its spindle. The message was brief, without explanation: "Army moving to Libnah."

The Rabshakeh stared at the parchment and then at the courier. "What does this mean?"

"I don't know. I've been away on another mission, and my superior sent me with this message."

"Was Lachish captured?" the cupbearer asked in puzzlement.

"I really don't know." The courier shifted position nervously. "I didn't get close enough to see. All I know is that the army was in great haste to go somewhere."

"To Libnah?" the Rabshakeh volunteered.

"I guess so.'"

Turning to the Tartan, the Rabshakeh commanded, "Take the troops to Libnah. Perhaps Lachish fell sooner than we expected."

"I don't think anyone will mind the change," the field marshal commented. "Libnah is closer than Lachish."

"You're right," the eunuch interjected. "And today will be a scorcher." The shouts of platoon sergeants and the tramp of tens of thousands of marching feet soon filled the air. The Assyrian army was again on the move—a living, breathing, shapeless mass, heading to the southwest . . . bound for Libnah. Many hours passed before the last enemy troops disappeared over the hills in the distance.

Arriving at Libnah, the Rabshakeh bowed before Sennacherib as slaves did before their masters. It mattered little that he was the highest official of the empire. All Assyrians were slaves of the great king.

Sennacherib motioned for him to rise. "What did Hezekiah answer?"

"The Jew refused to surrender, and the people follow him. They wouldn't talk with us." The cupbearer scratched his head. "I fear that nothing but a siege will sway them."

"That mangy dog!" The Assyrian monarch's anger mounted. "When I finish with him, Jerusalem will be a deserted field of rubble."

The king briefed his cupbearer on the events of the past week. The army had finished the siege at Lachish and moved on to Libnah. "But my scouts tell me of the approach of a large Egyptian army. I'd wager my throne that they're coming to aid Hezekiah." Sennacherib stood and paced to the brow of the hill overlooking Libnah. His troops had already started raising siege ramps against the walls. He could see volleys of arrows descending upon his soldiers and bouncing off their shields.

"Egypt is coming to protect Hezekiah all right," he said, facing the Rabshakeh. "But we will stop that." The king glanced back at Libnah. "I'm afraid we'll have to interrupt this siege to fight them. But there'll be plenty of time to capture Libnah."

For a long time the two admired the skill with which their soldiers worked. Siege warfare had become a science. The king and his cupbearer had seen it done hundreds of times, yet they marveled at the precision and horrible beauty of the scene.

An hour slipped by before either realized it. Suddenly the king broke the silence. "We need to let Hezekiah know that we will not permit him to link with Egypt." For a moment he was lost in thought. "I know. I'll send a letter to Hezekiah, demanding surrender. I'll make it stronger than before. That Jew must understand that this is his last chance for a peaceful settlement."

Sennacherib motioned to his scribe to begin writing. Occasionally he would pause to substitute a stiffer word or a harsher phrase. Within minutes the scribe handed him the completed copy, bowed, and backed away.

The Assyrian monarch passed the scroll to the Rabshakeh with orders to deliver it to the king of Judah. "I'll send the army with you again so that Hezekiah cannot link his troops with Egypt. I will stay here and wait for Pharaoh. Let's see how Hezekiah gets out of this."

Picturing the outcome, Sennacherib laughed. He would dispatch the Egyptians in short order, then join the Rabshakeh at Jerusalem, and he would personally destroy Hezekiah for good.

A Letter From Yahweh

Once again the Assyrian army surrounded the capital city, and the cupbearer stood in the highway beside the fuller's field. This time he did not request to speak with Hezekiah or his envoys. Only a sharp command: "Deliver this letter to your king."

A defending soldier lowered a small basket, an Assyrian placed the letter into it, and it vanished up the wall. No one dared open the leather pouch, for it was addressed to the king and sealed with the Assyrian seal. But everyone knew its contents—another threat.

The men on the wall wondered why the Assyrians consumed so much time sending messages back and forth. "Why are they stalling?" they asked each other. "Are they afraid to attack? What prevents them from beginning the siege?" Only God and the enemy knew.

Sennacherib's letter reached Hezekiah in his bedchamber. His heart skipped a beat when he saw it. With trembling hands he opened the pouch, unrolled the scroll, and read the message, written in Hebrew: "Do not let your God on whom you trust deceive you when He says: 'Jerusalem shall not fall to Assyria.' You have learned what the kings of Assyria have done to every country. None of the gods of the other nations have helped them. Are you likely to be spared?"

Without a word, Hezekiah walked slowly toward the Temple. The Assyrian had gone too far—he had challenged the living God to stop him. Only Yahweh could answer it.

The king knelt in his customary place of prayer. Unrolling the letter again, he spread it open. "Yahweh, God of Israel," he prayed, "You alone are God of all the earth, for You made heaven and earth. Give ear, and listen. Open Your eyes, and see. Sennacherib has sent this letter to insult You. It is true that Assyria has exterminated all the nations; they have thrown their gods into the fire, for they were not gods at all. But now, Yahweh, save us from his hand. Let all the kingdoms of the earth know that You alone are the one true God."

Hezekiah remained silently on his knees, realizing that the battle rested in God's hands and that he need no longer concern himself with it. While Hezekiah knelt, someone approached him. The king glanced up. "Your majesty," the man said, "Isaiah sends you this message: 'Yahweh says this: "I have heard your prayer." Here is a letter that Yahweh sends to the great king.'"

Reverently Hezekiah unrolled the scroll, realizing that Isaiah must have written it to him before he had entered the Temple. Then the king read it aloud. "The virgin daughter of Zion despises you. She tosses her head at you. You have insulted the Holy One of Israel! Through your envoys you have said: 'With my chariots I have climbed mountains; I have felled forests of cedars; I have dug wells and have dried up all the rivers of Egypt.'

"Do you hear? Long ago I planned it; and now I carry it out. Your part in my plan was to bring down fortified cities into heaps of ruins. Their inhabitants were like plants of the field. But I am there whether you rise or sit; I know whether you go out or come in. Because you have raved against me, and because your insolence has come to my ears, I will put my ring through your nostrils, my bit between your lips. I will make you return to Assyria by the road on which you came."

At the end Hezekiah noticed something addressed to himself. "This shall be a sign for you: This year you will eat the self-sown grain; next year you will eat that which sprouts in the fallow. But in the third year you shall sow and reap, plant vineyards, and eat their fruit. The surviving remnant of Judah shall bring forth new roots below and new fruits above; for a remnant shall go out from Jerusalem and survivors from Mount Zion. The jealous love of Yahweh shall accomplish all this.

"But the king of Assyria will not enter this city, he will let fly no arrow against it, confront it with no shield, and throw up no earthwork against it. By the road on which he came he will return. It is Yahweh who speaks. I will protect this city and save it."

A sense of complete peace overwhelmed Hezekiah. He had no more need to mourn, for divine help was at hand. Jerusalem was safe.

Calling for a messenger, Hezekiah sent the letter to the king of Assyria. Soon he would see how Yahweh would deliver Jerusalem.

The Angel of Death

The sun was past mid-heaven when Hezekiah's courier appeared on the wall. The Rabshakeh had paced back and forth before his tent, shouting insults at the city's defenders. As the day grew warmer, his temper flared even more violently.

Now the basket descended from the tower. The cupbearer's hopes rose. "Perhaps the king has decided to surrender, and we can go home," he mentioned to the Rabsaris as he indicated for an aide to get the letter. "This crazy war has lasted far too long."

It required but a minute for the Rabshakeh's servant to fetch the letter and but two for him to read it. As he scanned the scroll his face turned crimson. The Rabsaris, sitting calmly under the tree, was frightened to his feet by the Rabshakeh' s reaction.

"Who does that dog think he is?" the cupbearer roared, throwing the letter to the ground. Doesn't he know I can destroy him?" Systematically he cursed Hezekiah, Yahweh, and everyone in Jerusalem. "The siege begins tomorrow," he yelled in the direction of the city. "You've had your last chance!" Shaking his fist, he promised, "When we conquer you, we'll cut you in pieces. We'll defile your women and kill your children. Should anyone escape, they will become slaves!"

Furiously the Rabshakeh rerolled the scroll and returned it to its pouch, ordering the nearest messenger to take it to the king. "Tell him that I begin the siege tomorrow."

The courier disappeared, and the cupbearer faced the

Tartan. "Get the men ready," he barked at the officer. "We commence the siege tomorrow."

Orders flew around the city, and the soldiers began setting up camp. Tents went up, soldiers guarded the escape routes, and campfires were lit.

As the sun sank, the Rabshakeh made one more speech. Again he warned that neither Hezekiah nor Yahweh nor the Egyptian army could save the people from Sennacherib.

At last darkness, punctuated only by the light of thousands of fires, blanketed the landscape. Laughter and singing wafted through the air from small groups of men gathered around the campfires. The sparkle of fires expanded to the distant hills and blended with the stars to create a continuous twinkling from the foot of Jerusalem's walls up to the zenith.

Inside the city its nervous inhabitants went about their chores, eating their evening meals, and preparing for bed. Soldiers made final preparations for the defense that would begin at dawn. Wives and children attempted to encourage each other, trying to hide the dread they felt. Everyone from prophet and king down to the beggar in the street knew that unless Yahweh intervened, few of them would survive. And those who did would wish they hadn't.

In one home a soldier-father crouched before the fire, sharpening and polishing his sword. His wide-eyed son looked on, awed by his father's weapon.

"Do you plan to use that sword to kill Assyrians?" the boy asked.

"Yes, son . . . if they break into the city. But I hope it won't be necessary. In fact, if what Isaiah said is true, the Assyrians will never even start the siege."

"Really?"

"That's right, son." The man tested the newly sharpened edge.

"What did Isaiah say?"

"This morning, when I was in the Temple, the king was praying." The man paused, lowering the sword and staring at his son. "A messenger brought him a note from the prophet."

"What did the note say, Father?"

"I didn't hear all of it, but I did hear that Sennacherib will go back home in shame. In fact, he won't even come to Jerusalem."

"Father, do you believe that Yahweh will really save Jerusalem?"

"Yes, son." The man watched the flickering flames.

"Then, Daddy . . . why are you sharpening your sword?"

Startled, the man opened his mouth to speak, then closed it again. Did he really believe the prophet? he wondered to himself. Did he really have faith in Yahweh's power?

For a long time he studied the fire as he thought about all the power and goodness of his God, of His ability to save by many or by few . . . or completely by Himself, if He chose. He glanced at the sword that had occupied his attention for better than an hour. Then he shoved the weapon into its scabbard and tossed it into the corner. The sudden clatter frightened the family dog out of its dreams with a yip.

"That's a good question, son." He put his arm around the boy as the dog settled down again. The two gazed into the fire as Mother finished her chores before bedtime. Finally the father broke the long silence. "Son, . . . I believe that to-morrow we shall see the salvation of Yahweh."

Sennacherib felt restless as the sun set behind Libnah. "All the evidence I have," he said, "indicates that the Egyptians are approaching. And yet we have waited all day without a sign of them." The king scratched his chin through his curly beard.

"Our scouts saw them coming up the main road from Gaza," a general assured him.

"I wish they'd get here. I can't concentrate on Libnah

until I send them back toward the Nile." For the hundredth time that day he paced toward the brow of the hill. "Where are they? They should have been here by noon, but there's no sign of them."

A courier arrived from Jerusalem, and the king smiled. Ten years ago a message like this signaled Hezekiah's surrender. "Maybe the old dog has given up again."

But he couldn't believe his ears. Instead of surrender, Hezekiah actually threatened that Yahweh would send him home in shame. Grabbing the scroll, he hurled it at the royal tent. "Curses on Hezekiah!" he stormed. "Go now," he ordered another messenger. "Take two men with you. Tell the Rabshakeh to begin the siege at once."

It was the longest night the people of Jerusalem could remember. The streets were deserted, and few people stirred in their homes. It seemed too quiet for the watchmen. Night was a tense time for them. Who could tell if a movement came from friend or foe or foliage?

As the fingers of dawn grasped at the stars, everyone breathed more easily. Long before the sun peeped over the Mount of Olives, the wall swarmed with soldiers. But all remained quiet in the enemy camp. "That's odd," an archer said. "Their campfires have all gone out."

"I noticed," his officer replied. "And they haven't left their tents yet." He scanned the camp. "I was told they start a siege as soon as it gets light. They must be getting lazy."

Suddenly a cry sounded from the southwestern corner of the wall, and all eyes turned that way. Three riders—messengers—appeared on the horizon. "Now we'll see some action," someone muttered. "These men will wake somebody up."

The horsemen picked their way through the camp to the Rabshakeh's tent. They dismounted beside the tree and glanced around hesitantly. Approaching the tent, they seemed reluctant to enter unannounced. After a conference under the tree, one of the men peeked into the Rabshakeh's tent, then shrugged. For the time being they apparently decided to wait under the tree. The Rabshakeh was asleep.

More than an hour later they concluded they had better awaken the cupbearer. Something was wrong. Why wasn't anyone awake? One of the men entered the tent. Suddenly he screamed and rushed from the tent in fright. Stopping by the tree, he stammered out what he had seen.

The messengers raced from tent to tent, each time emerging with increasing fear. Soon they leaped on their horses and galloped over the hill.

Word quickly spread through Jerusalem. "The Assyrians are still asleep, and their messengers can't wake them up." When the news reached Hezekiah, he exclaimed, "This is the miracle Yahweh promised." As he spoke he headed for the wall. "The angel of death has stricken them while they slept."

Hezekiah studied the tents sprawled over the hills. "Perhaps we should send some scouts out to have a look." Quickly the patrol discovered that every Assyrian was dead. They all lay in eternal sleep, from the Tartan and the Rabshakeh down to the servant boys and the cooks. Yahweh's angel of death had stricken the entire Assyrian force.

Thousands streamed through the gates to see the sight. Military leaders organized the people to bury the dead and gather the weapons and valuables. It would take several days, but everyone gave thanks to Yahweh.

Sennacherib rose early, concerned about the Egyptians. "Send out more scouts," he ordered. "Perhaps they marched around us to join Hezekiah. That must not happen!" As the morning progressed he wondered why the messengers had not returned from Jerusalem. Irritated, he scolded the chief of the messenger service for the inefficiency of his men. "Why should the king be kept waiting like this? I shall devise a special torture for those who cause me this inconvenience!"

Toward noon three horses galloped toward his tent. Before they halted, he knew that they had come from Jerusalem. The men seemed greatly agitated. Had something gone wrong?

The story spilled out. "We came to the camp, and everyone appeared to be asleep." Hysterically the terrified man related his experiences. "We waited for more than an hour for the Rabshakeh to wake up. But when we entered to get him up . . ." The courier paused in terror.

"Come on, man," the king shouted. "What did you find?"

"He was dead!" The messenger's voice rose to a high-pitched wail. "We didn't find any wounds. He died in his sleep. And when we checked the other tents, we saw the same thing! Your majesty"—he sobbed now—"the entire army is dead . . . dead . . . not one survivor!"

Sennacherib's face paled, and he could scarcely breathe. The words that he had so scornfully heard the night before—the letter he had thrown against the wall of his tent—now returned to his mind. "I will put my ring through your nostrils, I will put my bit between your lips, to make you return by the road on which you came." And now this!

Trembling uncontrollably, the king tried to speak, then sank to his knees, at last falling on his face. What further calamity could happen now? "Yahweh is the God of heaven and earth!" he moaned. "Let's get out of here before we all die!"

His servants had stood paralyzed until now. Suddenly they sprang into action. Some helped the king to his feet. Others spread the word that they must depart for home immediately. Still others began packing equipment.

But the king ordered an immediate retreat. "Leave the tents and equipment!" he shouted. Without another word, he leaped into his chariot, with his armor-bearer and driver, and raced for home. In panic the surviving army dashed toward Assyria, north to Haran, then east to Nineveh. Hundreds died of hunger, thirst, disease, and sunstroke during the march. The Assyrian power over Judah had been broken. Sennacherib would never return again.

In Jerusalem, with the work of burying the dead finished and the booty collected, the people headed for the Temple to thank Yahweh for His salvation. They joined Isaiah in a song of deliverance:

> "God is renowned in Judah,
>   his name is great in Israel;
>   his tent is pitched in Salem,
>   his home is in Zion;
>   there he has broken the lightning-swift arrow,
>   the shield, the sword and the line of battle.
>
> "You the Illustrious and Majestic:
>   mountains of spoil have been captured;
>   heroes are now sleeping their last sleep,
>   the warriors' arms have failed them;
>   at your reproof, God of Jacob,
>   chariot and horse stand spellbound.
>
> "You the Terrible! Who can oppose you
>   and your furious onslaught?
>   When your verdicts thunder from heaven,
>   earth stays silent with dread;
>   when God stands up to give judgment
>   and to save all the humble of the earth.
>
> –Ps. 76:1-9, Jerusalem

Epilogue

Hezekiah lived for two or three years after the great victory. One of the finest kings of Judah, he built several cities, constructed the tunnel and Pool of Siloam, and erected the second wall. In spite of the cancerous taxes of Assyria, he gathered much wealth for Judah. His greatest service was the restoration of the Temple services and the religious reformation that followed.

His mistakes cost Judah dearly, however. If he had followed Isaiah's counsel and remained loyal to Assyria, Sennacherib probably wouldn't have invaded Palestine twice or deported more than 200,000 people. But then we would never have known God's mighty power to stop the most efficient war machine of that era.

Hezekiah's blunder with the Babylonian ambassadors eventually cost Judah its freedom. In 605 B.C., just 80 years after Hezekiah's death, Nebuchadnezzar conquered Judah and eventually destroyed Jerusalem.

Even so, when Hezekiah died, Judah mourned for many days, for his people greatly loved him.

Isaiah served more than 60 years under five of Judah's kings—Uzziah, Jotham, Ahaz, Hezekiah, and probably Manasseh. Often he told of his call to the prophetic ministry. He had been in the Temple praying when, in vision, he saw the Most High and received the summons to carry God's messages to His people.

His inspired testimony eventually cost him his life.

Siege at the Gates

Manasseh hated Isaiah because of his influence over Hezekiah. Tradition states that when Manasseh became sole ruler of Judah at the age of 22, he condemned Isaiah to death because he claimed to have seen God. The young king quoted Exodus 33:20, which stated that no man can see God and live. The passage gave him the excuse he wanted to have the old prophet executed. Manasseh ordered his men to place Isaiah in a hollow log and saw it in half.

Shebna, after his demotion, continued to build his extravagant tomb and ride in his chariot. But, true to prediction, the former steward was later captured and taken prisoner to a strange land—along with his chariot. He died on foreign soil. Archaeologists have discovered a tomb on the Mount of Olives that bears his name. As nearly as they can tell, the tomb has never been occupied.

Sennacherib was perhaps the most powerful of all the Assyrian kings. He and the other rulers of his nation greatly benefited the world of their time. They ended most local wars, provided an efficient central government and built good roads. Usually they allowed each country to govern itself as long as the nation paid its taxes.

But their inhuman acts have filled many volumes, and the cruelty shown by both kings and soldiers alike has rarely been equaled—even in twentieth-century concentration camps.

Sennacherib was the most cruel of the Assyrian kings. The king delighted in inventing new war machines and more efficient and painful methods of torture. He was hated by literally everyone outside Assyria, and many of his own people grew to detest him.

His unnecessary destruction of Babylon utterly severed him from the affection of his world. Several of the lists of kings drawn up by historians in his time left his name out entirely.

Unable to trust the historians to tell the story his way, he hired his own scribes to depict everything in ways that would favor him. At times his forces went down to terrible defeat in battle, but he would have his scribes write the account as though it were a victory. Often he would leave out a key event if it didn't suit his image. Perhaps that is why we have no record from him of anything he did during his last eight years. Never recovering from the blow he received in Judah at the hands of Yahweh, he didn't mention that campaign and remained silent after that.

In the month of Nisanu (late March or early April) of the year 681 B.C., while Sennacherib worshipped in the temple of Nisroch, his god, two of his sons, Adrammelech and Sharezar, crept up behind him and murdered him with a sword. They hoped to take over his throne. But their brother Esarhaddon prevented them from doing so.

The assassins fled for their lives to Armenia, and Esarhaddon assumed the throne. Thus ended the life of one of history's greatest, and perhaps most evil, kings—exactly in the way Isaiah had predicted.

Collect all the Exciting Stories in the Gates Series

SIEGE AT THE GATES
The Story of Sennaacherib, Hezekiah and Isaiah
(released 2007)

THE TEMPLE GATES
Josiah Purges Judah's Idolatry
(released 2008)

FIRE IN THE GATES
The Drama of Jeremiah and the Fall of Judah
(released 2007)

GATE OF THE GODS
God's Quest for Nebuchadnezzar
(released 2008)

THE OPEN GATES
From Babylon's Ashes, Freedom for the Jews
(released 2008)